TRAPPED

BETWEEN THE LASH AND THE GUN

Arvella Whitmore

TRAPPED
BETWEEN THE LASH AND THE GUN

A
Boy's
Journey

DIAL BOOKS

New York

Published by Dial Books
A member of Penguin Putnam Inc.
345 Hudson Street
New York, New York 10014

Copyright © 1999 by Arvella Whitmore
All rights reserved
Designed by Debora Smith
Printed in the U.S.A. on acid-free paper
First Edition
3 5 7 9 10 8 6 4

Library of Congress Cataloging in Publication Data
Whitmore, Arvella.
Trapped between the lash and the gun: a boy's journey
by Arvella Whitmore.—1st ed.
p.   cm.
Summary: Twelve-year-old Jordan is becoming dangerously
involved with a street gang when he is suddenly transported
through time to become a slave on the plantation of his ancestors.
ISBN 0-8037-2384-9
[1. Slavery—Fiction. 2. Afro-Americans—Fiction.
3. Time travel—Fiction.] I. Title.
PZ7.W598Sl   1999
[Fic]—dc21   98-14564   CIP   AC

To the Tuesday Writers' Group and to my grandchildren—Page and Nelson Whitmore, Claire and Charles Whitmore, Paul and Madeline Ranum.

ONE

Twelve-year-old Jordan leaned against the fridge drinking a Coke while his little sister, Tachelle, sat at the kitchen table munching on a cookie. A foggy mix of fear and longing swirled around Jordan as he watched Mom wrap a cup in newspaper, then carefully place it in a big cardboard box.

"I don't know why you want to move to that honky suburb," Jordan told his mother.

"Jordan, you know how I feel about that word," she said. "And besides, black folks are moving into Springdale all the time. Someday you'll thank me for moving this family to a place where there's less crime so you don't get mixed up with the wrong people." Mom's big dark eyes, slightly tilted up at the corners, flashed fire, and to Jordan that was a warning. Did she suspect? She'd have a fit if she knew who his new friends were, especially King, the Cobras' top man.

"Jordan," she said, "you're going to be grounded until doomsday if you skip any more classes. And I want to know why you're never here after school when I call from the office." Jordan guzzled Coke, tilting his head back to hide his face, feeling the bubbles sting his throat.

"Now you look at me, Jordan," she said, "and talk straight for a change."

He set his drink can down hard. It was his turn to attack. "Mom, you're in my face all the time and I'm tired of it."

His mother stared at him and her eyes filled with tears. "Oh, Jordan, sometimes I wonder whatever happened to that sweet little boy you used to be."

Jordan felt sorry he'd made her cry, but couldn't let it show. "I'm not a little boy anymore!" he said.

Mom stood there studying him. "No, you're not a little boy anymore, but I don't like the changes I see. I'm hoping that the move to Springdale will make a difference."

Tachelle got up and threw her arms around Mom's waist. "I just love the new house, Mama. I want the bedroom with the yellow wallpaper."

Mom sighed and hugged her. "We'll see! You and your brother may have to draw straws." Draw straws! Mom just assumed he'd be moving, but Jordan knew he never would.

The telephone rang and Tachelle ran to answer it.

Mom taped the box shut and Tachelle looked up from the phone. "Hey, Mom! Janey wants me to come over. Can I?"

"All right, since she's right next door, but I want you home by six." When Tachelle left, Jordan was dying to go too, but now that he and Mom were alone, he had some questions to ask her. He sat down at the table and finished his sister's snack.

Whenever Jordan tried to bring up the subject of his dad he felt as if he were trying to leap across a canyon that grew deeper each day. "Um, Mom, does Daddy know you bought that house?"

"Not yet."

"You going to tell him?"

"I guess so." But he knew she didn't want to.

"You ever going to get together again?"

She bit her lip and let out a long sigh. "Honey, no," she said in a quiet voice. "It just won't work. His easy money schemes drove me crazy. We're better off with him a thousand miles from here."

Her words cut through Jordan. He remembered how Daddy would grin at him and hug him and how he was always ready to play softball and take him fishing. Why didn't Mom ever think about those things? But Jordan also remembered lying awake nights listening to him and Mom fight. Then one day Daddy was gone and never came back. Jordan had begged Mom for airfare to visit him, but she'd always said no and wouldn't explain why. She had to be hiding something. But by hooking up with the Cobras, he'd soon be able to pay his own way and move in with Dad.

"I'm starting to grow tall and thin like Daddy, don't you think, Mom?" Getting her to talk about him was like pushing a huge rock up a steep hill.

"Yes, but I hope you don't turn out like him."

Jordan raged inside. It made him furious when Mom insulted Daddy. He stood up and slipped into his jacket, then put his baseball cap on back-ward the way every Cobra gang member did. "What's for dinner?"

"Thought I'd order a pizza."

"Great!" He walked to the door. "I'll be back."

"Where're you going?"

"Out." He was supposed to meet King in five minutes.

"Now you answer me straight, young man. Where exactly are you going?" Jordan didn't say a word and tried to wipe all expression off his face.

"For your information, Jordan, the sun went down five minutes ago, and those streets are no place for a kid after dark. And you'd better pull up those baggy pants of yours or they're gonna fall off."

"Stop sweatin' me, Mom!" He dashed outside and was racing down the porch steps when she opened the door and yelled, "Jordan! You be back here at six sharp! You hear me?" He didn't answer, just took off down the walk and headed for the stores on the corner. After he met with King, he planned to walk over to Grandpa's.

Jordan watched the shadows between the houses, scared of being jumped by a member of the Lobo gang. The enemy turf was always changing. Nobody around except some people getting off the bus. So far so good.

He felt bad about splitting with Mom and Tachelle. Part of him really wanted to move into that new house. But he'd made up his mind. It was just a few weeks ago that King had spotted him hanging around on the street and asked him if he wanted to make some easy bucks. He'd said, "Sure, why not?" thinking about airfare to see Daddy, not some lifelong vow. Lately he'd been sort of lonely after school, and hanging out with the Cobras was exciting. At first he felt guilty about some of the things they wanted him to do, but he got used to it. Then after the crew took him in, some of the guys made it clear that there was no getting out. If he moved to Springdale, only a few miles away, he had a pretty good idea what would happen to him—and maybe even Mom and Tachelle. He'd heard about this one Cobra who had tried to quit. His name was Joey. He was still around—in a wheelchair. But that wouldn't happen to Jordan. After all, Mom had said Daddy lived "a thousand miles away." He'd be okay living with him.

Packer, the guy who camped out in an empty house down on Tucker Avenue, might take him in until he could earn enough for an airline ticket. Mom would hunt for him, but after a while she'd give up the way Packer's mom did. In spite of her nagging, Jordan knew he'd miss Mom. He was proud of her for getting that good job in Springdale. And he'd miss Tachelle too. For a sister, she was okay.

A gust of wind rattled dead leaves along the sidewalk. Jordan huddled into his jacket, suddenly aware that November wasn't a good month to start living on the streets.

"Hey, Slick!" Jordan stopped and listened. Straight ahead, behind a tall fence, King was calling his Cobra name in a half-whisper. Jordan's breath came fast with excitement and fear. Pleasing King was important. He popped out of the shadows and fell into step with Jordan. The street lamp threw a halo around King's cornrow hair, and the eighteen-carat chains around his neck flashed gold. The cellular phone that hung on his belt buzzed. To Jordan, he was *the* coolest.

King picked up the phone. "Call back. I'm busy." Jordan thought King's gang name suited him. He was twenty years old and knew every-thing.

"The meeting's all set for tonight," said King. "Six sharp. Baker's parking lot. Bring the money, and don't be late."

"I'll be there," Jordan said, "with the money." The Cobras were setting it up for him to buy a gun. Every Cobra had to be "strapped"; that is, he had to carry a gun for protection, and Jordan couldn't wait.

"Where you headed now, bro?" King asked.

Jordan didn't want to tell him he was going to Grandpa's because he didn't want to sound like some stupid little kid.

"Just hanging out." Jordan's voice shook; King rattled his nerves no matter how cool he tried to act. It was partly because he looked up to him and partly because he was more than half afraid of him.

"Just hangin', huh? What's happenin', cuz?"

"Nothing." He hated lying right then because everybody knew King could smell a lie six blocks away.

"Saw the enemy's mark on the Conner apart-ments," King said. "Watch it. We don't want to lose one of our best runners. You gonna be down, man." Jordan felt proud, because being "down" was an honor. Mom made him feel like a dumb little kid, but King made him feel grown-up, like a real man.

King stopped and grabbed Jordan's arm. "What's wrong, homeboy?" Jordan wondered how he knew something was bothering him, and whether he should spill his troubles. Why not? King was on his side, wasn't he? Like his dad or an older brother would have been.

"It's my mom," he said.

"She hasslin' you for skippin' school?"

"Yeah. And I'm going to need a place to crash."

"She kick ya out?"

"No. Bought a house in Springdale. Has a job there."

King whistled under his breath. "Springdale, huh? She goin' high class, man. You ain't leavin' too?"

"Nope." No way would he tell him about moving a thousand miles away.

King grinned. "Yeah, man. You got the right idea there. So don't sweat it, you hear? You can move in with me and my girlfriend. Temporary, o' course."

Jordan was stunned by King's offer and more

than a little thrilled. To refuse would be unthinkable, but all he said was, "What if my mom tries to find me?"

"Listen, Slick, you ain't the first one we hid. We got ways and we got means your mama ain't never heard of."

King's words soothed Jordan's mind. He should have known all along that the Cobras would take care of him. King patted him on the back, then turned and walked off. Jordan realized he hadn't felt like this since before Daddy had walked out. Complete. Like he belonged to something he could count on. The Cobras were his family now, at least for a while. He felt free and strong. "See you at six," he called out.

TWO

Jordan had a secret reason for dropping by to see Grandpa that evening. After letting Jordan in, the old man sat down in his recliner and tilted it back. Every table and chair in the room was stacked with magazines and newspapers. Even the radiators were piled high. People in the neighborhood, knowing what a reader Grandpa was, brought him old ones. Jordan was in a hurry, but knew he had to spend a little time gabbing about this and that to make it seem like an ordinary visit.

"Hear your mama bought that house," Grandpa said.

"Yeah."

"You don't seem too keen on it. What's the matter? Don't you like it?"

"It's nice." Jordan forced a smile. He didn't want to talk about the new house, or Springdale or Mom and Tachelle right then. He'd made his choice. Suddenly he just wanted to back out the door and run, but he knew he had to stay to carry out his plan.

"How are you doing in school, young man?"

"Okay, I guess." School! Another thing he didn't want to talk about. For Mom and Tachelle it had always been a breeze. He wasn't in their league when it came to schoolwork. And Grandpa was worse than Mom, always pushing him to study and making him feel dumb. Grandpa just couldn't understand people who didn't like school. As far as he was concerned, skipping classes and dropping out entirely, the way Jordan planned to do, was a crime. This conversation was drifting into uneasy territory, making him feel trapped and on edge.

"What's your favorite subject?" Grandpa asked.

What could he say when he hated them all? "Uh, history, I guess."

"You guess? Don't you know? What are you studying now?"

Jordan looked at the wall clock. He had to get out of here. "Oh, oh, Grandpa! I just remembered! I have to run. I promised Mom I'd be home by six." Lying was getting easier now—that is, with everyone except King. He wouldn't dare lie to him. "Mind if I use the bathroom before I go?"

"Help yourself, but jiggle the handle after you flush."

"Okay, Grandpa." On the way Jordan walked into the bedroom. Since Grandpa had grown up during the Great Depression and didn't trust banks, his family often laughed and said that he probably hid his money under his mattress. Grandpa himself claimed he always "kept a little something around for a rainy day." Jordan, his eyes on the door, knelt and lifted the bedcovers. He ran his hands between the mattress and box springs as far as he could reach. Nothing. He went around to the other side of the bed and did the same. No money. He searched the dresser drawers, quietly digging through Grandpa's underwear, socks, and shirts. There were a few small bills in an old shaving mug, but not enough to bother taking. Jordan swore under his breath. Then something caught his eye. Sitting there on the dresser, between two stacks of old *National Geographics*, was Grandpa's treasured keepsake. He lifted the lid of the little square white box. Lying inside on a wad of yellowed old cotton was an ancient pocket watch. Jordan remembered how Grandpa was always going on about how "precious" it was. On the watch's cover an artist had engraved a tiny picture of a Southern mansion, a beautiful house with a row of columns across its front. Etched gold, Grandpa had called it. If it was real gold, it could be worth a bundle. Written in a fancy scroll under the house picture was the word "Hilltop." Tiny flowers and leaves circled the house like a wreath. Jordan had to admit it was beautiful. He ran his fingers over it.

Every Christmas and Thanksgiving, for as long as Jordan could remember, Grandpa had taken the watch out of his pocket and told the history of it to anybody who'd listen. It was some long story about how it was more than 150 years old and had belonged to one of his "forebears," the word Grandpa always used. Then there was some more stuff about his great-great-grandfather, who had been a slave, and how he had run away from a Southern cotton plantation. Grandpa loved family history more than anything. To Jordan, it was just some moldy old story about people who didn't have anything to do with him.

Jordan had mixed feelings about taking something from Grandpa that meant so much to him. But he had often heard him say that the watch would be his someday anyhow. With that thought in mind, he buried his guilty feelings and slipped the watch and its thick gold chain into his jeans pocket. Grandpa wore it only on special occasions, and with the box still there on his dresser, it would be a while before he missed it. In a few minutes Jordan could sell the watch at the pawnshop and have the money he needed. If he was careful and did what the Cobras wanted, maybe he'd even have the cash to buy it back and return it before Grandpa noticed it was gone.

He made a big thing of flushing the toilet and jiggling the handle. When he came out, Grandpa was getting up out of his recliner.

"Bye, Grandpa."

"Stay awhile, Jordan. We can phone your mama."

"Can't tonight. She ordered a pizza."

"Shucks. I wanted to show you the new genealogy chart cousin Ned sent me. His fancy computer spits out ancestors faster than a chewing gum factory. He printed out all the known descendants of Uriah Henning."

"Uriah Henning?"

"You remember. The first black owner of the Hilltop watch. Your great-great-great-great-grandfather. Might even make a good history project for school."

Jordan's throat tightened. Of all the times to bring up the watch! He had to beat it, and fast.

"Sure," he said on his way out the door, "show it to me the next time I come." He tried to sound casual enough to hide his jitters, and at the same time seem politely interested. But Jordan thought Grandpa was a little weird for wasting his time on such a stupid hobby. What point was there in studying dead relatives?

On his way to Wagner's Pawn Shop, Jordan thought about what it would be like to move in with King for a month or so until he got that airline ticket. Talk about exciting! He walked without making a sound and studied all the shadows. No one on the street but a couple of women with shopping bags. All right so far. Nobody'd dare mess with him after he got strapped. No way, man.

Wagner's was on the other side of a street underpass several blocks away. Mom would kill him for going down into that underpass after dark because the homeless slept there sometimes. He walked on, watching all the shadows, wondering every minute if he was going through Lobo turf.

He walked faster, hearing the scrape of gold chain against watch. He couldn't help imagining what Grandpa's face would look like if he happened to open that little white box too soon. But Jordan couldn't afford to think about that now. He needed the money by six tonight. Besides, he was going to buy the watch back as soon as he could, wasn't he?

Jordan was heading into a poorer, more run-down part of town. Since there were more people on the street, he felt safer somehow. Up ahead he saw the entrance to the underpass. Soon he'd have the money in his pocket and wouldn't have to think about what he'd done to get it. There would be no turning back. Jordan started to run.

Just before going down the underpass, Jordan stopped by a street lamp, took the watch out of his pocket, and wound it. He'd be bound to get more money for a watch that worked. He set the time by the clock tower on the next block. Five-thirty. The watch's ticking seemed louder than normal. He stared at it, wondering if he should open the back and look at its gears. But what good would that do? He wouldn't know how to fix it. Kicking aside the trash and leaves that had collected on the sloping sidewalk, he hurried down the street underpass. The watch's ticking grew louder and pulsed against his hand. As Jordan started up the slanted sidewalk leading to the other side, the ticking became intense and throbbed inside his head. He shook the watch, hoping to silence it, but it ticked on.

The instant Jordan stepped up on the other side, the ticking stopped and everything looked strange. He had expected to find himself at the corner of Crane and Sutter streets. Wagner's Pawn Shop and the clock tower should have been just across the street, but the street was gone. Instead he was standing in a grove of trees.

And the watch was gone! Jordan stared at his empty palm. He must have dropped it. But why hadn't he felt it slip out of his hand or heard it fall? Looking down at his feet, he discovered that he was standing in tall weeds. Weeds? At Crane and Sutter? His scalp prickled. He had to find the watch. It had to be somewhere on the underpass sidewalk. Jordan spun around to retrace his steps, but everything was different. The underpass was gone. Trees stood all around him. Overhead, patches of daylight struggled through tangled branches. But how could that be? It was dark just a few minutes ago.

His stomach twisted itself into a painful knot and his knees felt weak. He was lost. Maybe he'd stumbled into one of the city parks. But he couldn't have! He'd gone down into the underpass, then up to the other side. He knew he had! He whirled around again, looking for familiar sights, but there weren't any. The clock tower and the street signs were gone. Come on now, Jordan, he told himself, streets and concrete underpasses don't just puff away into thin air. But it seemed that the whole city had disappeared. And so had the watch! He searched through the weeds near his feet, but it just wasn't there.

Panic squeezed his throat and his heart raced. He staggered through the underbrush, trembling and panting. Birds sang all around him. Shivers crawled up his spine, and he yelled "Help!" as loud as he could. A horse and buggy suddenly appeared and passed by him several yards away, but didn't stop.

"What was that?" Jordan shrieked.

A child's voice said, "Oh that be Dr. Byars callin' on sick white folk. He ain't nothin' to scare a body." The craziest-looking little black kid Jordan had ever seen stepped out from behind a big tree. He couldn't have been more than ten. He was barefoot and dressed in a shirt that came down to his knees and was made out of dirty burlap. It had no collar or buttons; just holes for his head and arms to go through. And his hair looked like somebody'd chopped it off with a hatchet. Jordan thought he might be some homeless street kid.

"Where am I?" Jordan asked him.

"You is in the swamp woods." The boy stretched his words out in a lazy drawl.

"Swamp woods! Talk sense, man," Jordan said. All of a sudden he noticed how hot it was. It didn't feel like November at all. He took off his jacket and tied the arms around his waist. "Where's the nearest street?"

"Ain't no streets 'round here."

Jordan didn't believe him. "What're you doing here anyway?"

"My masta send me out to find his watch."

"Your master?" Jordan wondered if it was just a coincidence that the boy happened to mention a watch. Why did Grandpa's watch tick so loud just before he found himself in these woods? And where was it now? Sweat rolled down his neck and his hands turned to ice. He had to find his way out of here! Right now, more than anything, he just wanted to go home and have pizza with Mom and Tachelle. And since he'd lost the watch, he didn't dare show up at Baker's parking lot. King would kill him.

"Hey, kid!" Jordan said. "Tell me how to get back to Crane and Sutter streets."

"I don't know what you talkin' about."

Jordan grabbed him by the neck of his raggedy shirt.

"Don't you hold out on me! I gotta get home."

The kid was cool. "Careful where you step," he said, "snakes everywhere. And if you hears horses and dogs, hide."

Jordan sneered at him, then let him go. Snakes! Horses and dogs! What a crazy kid. Jordan turned around, straining to see something he knew, but nothing looked familiar. The sounds of birds had replaced the roar of traffic. And all he could see was the kid in the sack shirt and the dark steamy woods all around him. Vines and wisps of something that looked like grayish-green witch's hair hung from the tree branches. Thinking that he'd surely lost his mind, Jordan felt a stab of fear shoot clear through him.

THREE

"Hey, I gotta get back!"
Jordan's voice broke, then came out in a squeak. His knees trembled. The kid followed him as he stepped and clawed through thick underbrush. When he pricked his fingers on some thorns and saw blood, he yelled, "Let me outta here!"

"Shhh!" the kid said. "They'll hear you. Hush up!"

"Who?"

"The paddyrollers."

Jordan felt like shaking him. Maybe then his words would unscramble themselves and come out straight. "What's a paddyroller? Talk sense, man."

"They's the poor whites keepin' an eye on us slaves, so we doesn't run away."

"I don't believe you. You're tryin' to mess with me!" Either this kid was crazy or else *he* was. "There's no such thing as slaves!" Jordan yelled. He fought for breath. Panic was smothering him.

"We is all slaves," the kid said, "and you better duck behind that big tree yonder, 'cause I hears 'em comin', and if you ain't got no pass, you is in big trouble."

"What do you mean, 'no pass'?"

"You gotta have a note from the masta sayin' you got a right to be off his place. And if you don't have one, the paddyrollers'll take you back for a whippin'."

His explanation sounded a little like the turf wars between the Lobos and the Cobras. Jordan thought he must be having a bad dream. Not wanting to make things any worse, he did what the kid said and hid behind a fat tree. Sure enough, he heard horses' hooves clop-clopping toward them and men talking. Jordan peeked out and saw three white men on horseback riding up a dirt path. They carried rifles and were plenty tough looking, like something straight out of a Wild West movie. They wore broad-brimmed straw hats and needed shaves. One of them stopped the kid and questioned him.

"Whose nigger are you?" The man had a yellow mustache and rode a gray horse. Jordan gritted his teeth. How dare he say that "n" word!

"I belongs to Masta Henning up at Hilltop," the kid told them.

Hilltop! Jordan's mouth fell open. Wasn't that the name of the house on Grandpa's watch? And Henning was Grandpa's last name and Jordan's own middle one! He shivered. Jordan, he told himself, this can't be happening. It *couldn't* happen! He wondered if he'd passed out on that underpass sidewalk. Maybe someone had hit him over the head, some thief or maybe a rival gang member. He'd better wake up soon.

"Hilltop, huh?" a dark-bearded man on a brown horse said. "Where's your pass, boy?" They didn't sound friendly. The kid reached into his pocket and handed him a card. The white man studied it, then looked down at him.

"What's your name, boy?"

"Uriah Henning."

Uriah Henning! Jordan remembered what Grandpa had said less than an hour before; that Uriah Henning was his great-great-great-great-grandpa's name, the slave who had owned the Hilltop watch! But this was crazy!

"What's your errand, boy?" asked the third white man.

"My masta done lost his watch and send me out to find it."

The watch! Jordan wondered if that watch had somehow cast a spell on him. He never should have touched it.

The third man handed the card back to Uriah. "Well, did you find it?"

"No, sir. Not yet, sir."

"Well, I reckon you'd better be gettin' back to your master."

"Yes, sir."

"Any other niggers with ya?" That word again. And spoken by a white man! Jordan clenched his fists. But the kid just stood there and took it.

"No, sir." The kid was a good liar. Looked and sounded so honest that you'd swear he was telling the truth.

"You better head on back to Hilltop then," said the first man. Uriah stood still, as if waiting for them to go.

"What you waitin' for, boy?" asked the dark-bearded one.

"Thought I'd do more searchin' 'round here.

Masta'll have me whipped if I don't find his watch."

The three men looked at one another, then the blond one said, "Just leave him be. He ain't too far from his master's place." All three rode on, and Jordan crept around the tree to stay out of sight.

Uriah waited until their sound faded away, then walked over to Jordan. "Help me find the watch," he said.

"What?"

"I done saved your skin. Help me find the watch."

The watch! "What does your master's watch look like?" Jordan asked.

"It's the most beautifullest watch I ever seen," he said. "It's gold and has a picture of the masta's house on the cover. And there's a wreath 'round it."

Grandpa's watch! Jordan tried to make sense of his situation. If the watch had brought him here, it could probably take him back. He had to get it. He looked all around. Nothing but trees and forest shadows.

"All right," Jordan said, pretending to play along, "where do you think he lost it?" Uriah led him to a puddle under a spreading tree; the branches looked like dark stretched-out arms. The puddle was pitch-black. Jordan put his hand into the shallow water and squeezed the mud through his fingers, but he felt nothing hard and round like a watch. If Uriah found it first, Jordan would have to take it away from him. It wouldn't be hard. Uriah was splashing water, pawing through the mud.

Jordan wondered if he was already late for the meeting at Baker's parking lot. King would never believe what had happened. When he got back, he'd have to make up some story to tell him. A good one too, because King could have him beat up if he thought he was lying.

"Find anything?" he asked Uriah.

"No."

"Keep digging," Jordan said.

Uriah stood up. "Can't. It's gettin' dark. The masta, he want me back before sundown."

"Oh, no you don't!" Jordan yelled. He'd probably found the watch and was trying to duck out. He roughed the kid up a little and searched him. No watch.

"Why you beatin' on me?" Uriah asked. "I ain't done nothin' to you. I gotta go back to the big house."

In a panic, Jordan shouted, "You can't leave me here!" He knew he wasn't acting the way a Cobra should, losing his cool like that. He was glad King couldn't see him. But no way would he spend the night by himself in these strange woods full of snakes and those paddyroller people.

"I gotta go." Uriah turned and headed toward the path where the three men had stopped him. Jordan decided to follow him. Before the kid could disappear, Jordan took off his baseball cap and hung it on a branch above the puddle to mark the place where the watch was supposed to be. He'd come back and find it as soon as he could. Then he caught up with Uriah.

"Hey," Jordan said, "you going to help me find the watch?"

"Why you want that watch so bad? It ain't yours."

"I had one just like it, only I lost it."

"I don't believe you. Ain't no other watch in the world like that one. Masta had it made special jus' for him."

"Then if it's so special," Jordan said, "we ought to find it. Let's come back here and look for it in the morning."

"Can't," he said. "Gotta go to work."

"Go to work? A little kid like you?"

"It's cotton-pickin' time. Gotta be out in the fields when the second horn blows."

Jordan didn't ask him what he meant by the "second horn" because he was too busy trying to understand what had happened. He figured that time had played a dirty trick on him, thanks to the watch. He'd found himself back in the 1800's somewhere, and this little kid was an ancestor of his, only he didn't know it, of course. How could he?

They walked for what must have been a mile or more. Uriah didn't say much, but Jordan thought that if he was putting on an act, it wouldn't take much to break him down.

"Hey, kid," he said, "what do you like to watch on TV?"

Uriah stopped and stared at Jordan with a blank face. "What you talkin' about?"

"Television."

"What's that?" If he was playacting, he was doing a great job. So much for television. Okay, so he never heard of it.

Just to make sure, Jordan tossed out another question. "Do you like rap?"

"What?"

"Rap. Rap music!"

"You talk funny. Don't make no sense."

Jordan grabbed his arm. "You know who I think you are?"

"Who?"

"My great-great-great-great-grandpa!"

The kid stared at Jordan. Then he started to giggle. Soon he was laughing so hard that he stopped to hold his sides. "You is crazy!" he gasped. "How can a chile like me be anybody's great-great-great-great-grandpappy?" Jordan was put off. The kid was making fun of him, but then he couldn't expect him to understand. Not for a while anyway. So Jordan decided to relax, go back to that tree in the morning, and try to find the watch. When Uriah started walking again, Jordan followed.

"Who you belong to?" Uriah asked.

"Nobody," Jordan said. But he knew that wasn't exactly true. He belonged to the Cobras, but how could he explain that to this kid who might as well be from another planet?

"You mean you's free?"

"Sure," Jordan said.

"I never seen a free nigger before. What's your name?"

"Jordan Henning Scott."

Uriah looked into his face and said, "You say your middle name be Henning?"

"Yeah. I was named after my Grandpa Henning."

"Maybe we is related in some way."

"Hey," Jordan said, "what's the date, anyway?"

"What you mean, date? What's a date?"

Jordan opened his mouth to explain, but Uriah interrupted.

"The masta, he don't let us slaves learn nothin'." He stopped and looked at Jordan, hard. "Do you know how to read and write?"

"Sure. Doesn't everybody?"

"Us slaves don't. Do you go to school like white folks?"

Jordan nodded.

"Where you from?"

"Up north," Jordan said. What good would it do to explain any more? The kid probably wouldn't believe him.

Uriah stopped, raised his shirt, and turned his back to Jordan. "See them stripes?"

When Jordan saw the big welts all across Uriah's back, some with fresh scabs on them, he felt sick. It looked as if somebody'd worked him over with a whip.

"What happened?"

"The masta's boy, he be teachin' me to read, and when his daddy caught him, the overseer done give me five lashes. I fainted dead away after the third, and when I woke up he done poured salt water on me. Then he give me another lash for screamin'. The masta, he be too refined to whip the slaves hisself, so he has the overseer do it."

Jordan's mouth fell open in disbelief. "What happened to his son?"

"Nothin'. He just don't teach me no more."

"You mean you got beat up just because you were learning to read?"

"Yessir. If you don't believe me, you just ask Ol' Joe. He the only nigger 'round here know how to read, only he keep it a secret. It be against the law for slaves to read. He say the whites made up that law 'cause they be scared that if we learns too much we be fightin' to get free. Ol' Joe, he be hidin' out in the swamp woods."

What the boy had said blew Jordan's mind, but

he just kept quiet and followed him into a clearing. He'd have to get that watch back—and the sooner the better. He was glad he'd remembered to mark the spot. But what if he couldn't find the tree where he'd hung his cap? He wasn't used to picking his way through a woods. A chill crept up his spine. He'd have to make Uriah go with him.

They were soon climbing a grassy hill. Jordan hoped that when they reached the top he'd be able to crawl out of this nightmare and see the streets he knew. No such luck. Standing in the distance was a beautiful mansion with huge trees and flowering bushes around it. Jordan knew at first glance that it was the real Hilltop; the etched picture on the watch had come to life. The setting sun cast a gold light on the tall, fat pillars marching across the front of the house. It was awesome. He just stood there, feeling weightless, as though he were swimming in a dream.

FOUR

"Hey, man, that's some house!" Jordan whispered. "What's it like inside?"

"I don't know," said Uriah. "I ain't never been in there."

"You mean to tell me that you work on this place and you've never been inside that house?"

"I is a field hand. Field slaves ain't allowed to go in the big house. Only the cooks and maids and manservants gets to go in there. But us field slaves, we doesn't like the house help. They's too uppity. They think they's special, and they spy on us field hands."

"But that's not fair!" Jordan said. "You ought to tell the master to let you go in that house."

"It ain't my place to tell the masta what to do."

"Well, if you won't, then I will."

"You better not."

"They can't hurt me. I'm free."

"That don't seem too likely," Uriah said.

Jordan wondered what he meant, but didn't ask.

Uriah stopped and stood in front of him. "You better not let nobody in the big house see you. They's gonna ask where you from, and if you can't answer straight off, the masta, he be sendin' you to the trader. If you is lucky, he might let you stay 'round here and work."

"Hey! Cut that out!" Jordan said. "I'm not a slave! Tomorrow morning you're going to take me back to that puddle and we're going to find that watch."

"I can't," Uriah said. "Like I tol' you, I is pickin' cotton from sunup to sundown."

"Can't you sneak out on your lunch hour?" Jordan asked.

"What you talkin' about, lunch hour?"

"Don't they give you an hour off for lunch? Everybody gets an hour off for lunch." The kid stared at Jordan as if he didn't understand plain English.

"Don't you get to eat in the middle of the day?" Even when Jordan asked the question in a different way, Uriah stared blankly at him. What was his problem anyway? Had the kid suddenly gone deaf? "Do you go home to eat?" Jordan spoke slow and loud, then in that same voice he said, "I was thinking you could skip lunch and run back to the woods with me then."

"We doesn't go home to eat," Uriah said. "We eats our corn cake in the field, and if we goes away we gets a whippin'. The overseer and the driver, they's watchin' us every minute, flickin' their whips."

Jordan finally got the picture and tried to push it out of his mind. "Then when *can* you lead me back to the woods?"

"When and if I gets another pass from the masta to look for his watch."

Jordan grabbed the neck of Uriah's shirt and said, "I'm going up to that house with you, and you'd better ask for a pass. If you don't, I'll give you a pounding you won't forget." Then he let Uriah go with a shove. The kid caught himself before he fell backward. Jordan felt ashamed of treating him that way, especially since he was younger than him, but the kid had to understand how desperate he was.

"You'll be sorry," Uriah said to him, "but come

on ahead then." Jordan followed Uriah to the big house but when he started up the broad steps to the front door, Uriah told him he couldn't do that.

"Why not?" Jordan asked.

"You just can't. That's why. We uses the back door."

"That's stupid!" Jordan said. Inside, he was boiling. Talk about screwed-up rules! Man! The kid led him all the way around the house to the back door. A couple of big hunting dogs sniffed at them and barked. The house was a lot bigger than it seemed from a distance. It was huge.

Uriah knocked, and a fat black woman dressed in a long gray dress and starched white apron came to the door.

"I be needin' to talk to the masta," said Uriah.

"He's havin' dinner. I'll take the message," said the woman. Just by the snooty way she stood in the doorway, blocking it, Jordan knew she wasn't about to let them in.

"Tell the masta I is back, and that I be wantin' a pass for tomorrow so I can finish what he tol' me to do."

She stretched out her hand. "Give me your pass, boy." When she took the card, she narrowed her eyes at Jordan. "Who's this?" she asked Uriah.

"My name's Jordan Henning Scott."

"Ain't nobody by that name on this place," she said. "What you doin' carryin' the masta's name?" Jordan didn't know what to say. How could he begin to tell his story to this woman with the stony face?

"He say he be free," Uriah explained.

The woman threw back her head and laughed. "There ain't no free niggers for miles around here. The overseer won't have no trouble whippin' the truth out of him."

Jordan wasn't about to let his back get scarred like Uriah's. He wanted to run. But to where? The only place he could go was into that forest with the snakes and those paddyrollers. No thanks. It made more sense to stick with Uriah. If he could get a chance to explain to the master that this was all a mistake, he'd probably understand and maybe even help him return to his own time. Besides, this had to be some kind of a bad dream, and the odds were he'd wake up soon. Relax, man, he told himself, just go with the flow.

"Wait here," the woman said to them. "The masta'll be wantin' to talk to you." Soon another black woman wearing a long white apron came out of a little building next to the house. She was tall and muscular and carried the biggest platter of fried chicken Jordan had ever seen. It made him so hungry that he felt as if he could eat the whole thing himself.

She walked toward the back door. "What you boys doin' hangin' 'round here?"

"I'm waitin' to see the masta 'bout a pass," said Uriah.

Jordan smacked his lips. That chicken smelled delicious. "Say," he said, "could you let us have a piece of that?"

The woman stopped and stared at them. "You is askin' me to get myself into one heap o' trouble. No sireee! I ain't about to take a whippin' for feedin' no field hands." She held the platter high, then turned to Jordan. "Where you from? I ain't seen the likes o' you 'round here." She looked at Uriah. "You know the masta don't allow no visitors callin' on his slaves. What's he doin' here?"

"I found him in the woods," said Uriah.

The big woman lowered the platter and shook her head. "You know you not supposed to bring runaways here. That be the paddyroller's job. I'll have to tell the masta on you."

"I couldn't help it," cried Uriah, "he followed me!"

So that's what they thought he was! A runaway! Jordan would have to set them straight.

"Open that door for me, boy," she told Uriah. "I gotta get this chicken in to the mistress before it get cold." There went the chicken, inside with the cook. Jordan felt so starved that he could have eaten his shoe.

Soon a white man with a big belly and a dinner napkin tucked under his double chin came to the door. When Uriah started to shake, Jordan knew that this had to be the master. It reminded him of the way he always shook whenever he saw King, no matter how cool he tried to act.

"So," said the man, "what can I do for you, Uriah?" He spoke in a kindly voice.

"Masta, I be needin' another pass." Uriah's voice quavered.

"We didn't find the watch," Jordan said. Uriah jabbed him in the ribs with his elbow, as if warning him to shut up.

The master looked at Jordan. "And just who are you, boy?"

"My name is Jordan Henning Scott."

"Jordan *Henning* Scott?" A puzzled look came over the man's face. Then he smiled. "You must be descended from one of the slaves my father sold when I was child. Where are you from?"

"Up north," Jordan said.

"Where up north?"

Jordan was struck dumb. How could he possibly make this man understand where he really came from?

"He say he be free," said Uriah.

"That remains to be seen," the man said. "By the way, how did you get here?"

At last Jordan had his chance to explain. "It was after dark and I was heading for this street underpass, see? With my grandfather's watch. When I started down under the street, the watch ticked real loud and didn't sound normal. And then . . ." He went on with his story, telling every detail. When he finished, Jordan glanced at Uriah, who squirmed and studied his bare toes. Jordan realized that it was the wildest-sounding story he'd ever heard. And judging from the amused look on Master Henning's face, Jordan was sure the man hadn't believed a word of it.

"Well, boy, I reckon I have more than a few doubts about your story, and I'll believe you're free when you show me your freedom papers.

You surely carry your freedom papers with you?"

"Freedom papers?" How was he supposed to know about freedom papers? Maybe he could fake it. Jordan searched in his pockets but all he could come up with was a gum wrapper and a wrinkled old library card Grandpa had insisted he sign up for. He'd used it once. He handed it to the man.

The master puzzled over the card and kept saying, "Very interesting. Very interesting, indeed. Public library!"

"It's where people go to read and borrow books," Jordan explained.

"Can't say I ever heard of a place like that. Certainly not a place where coloreds would be allowed."

Then he handed the card back to him. "Boy, I'm afraid this card is not a freedom paper. Whatever it is, I suspect it's stolen."

Stolen! Jordan could see that he wasn't getting anywhere with this guy. And to think that a few minutes ago he was actually counting on this man to help him.

"And," the master went on, "your clothes appear to be stolen too. Though I must admit I've never seen anybody with clothing quite like yours."

"Hey!" Jordan cried. "You got me all wrong, mister! My mom bought me these jeans and this shirt and jacket at a shopping mall, see? And that's the truth!"

The man chuckled and shook his head. "Boy, you hatch the queerest tales I ever heard. We'll have to regard you as a runaway until we can locate your owner. In the meantime you can stay in the slave quarters. I'll walk down there with you and ask Uriah's family to take you in. And I'll notify the overseer. You will be expected to work with our field hands starting tomorrow morning."

Jordan didn't say a word, but inside he was exploding. *He can't do this to me! He can't!*

"Masta," said Uriah, "I be needin' another pass to look for the watch." *The watch! It was Jordan's only hope.*

Master Henning smiled, reached behind his napkin, and drew the watch out of his vest pocket. *It couldn't be! But there it was!* The house on its cover caught the light and glowed in the setting sun.

"That won't be necessary," Master Henning said. "You see, I hadn't lost it in the woods after all. Dr. Byars dropped it by the house this evening. It seems I'd left it at his place yesterday afternoon when he examined me for my stomach complaint. Thoughtless of me."

A dark cloud of dread swept over Jordan. He could be doomed to a life of slavery forever unless he woke up from this nightmare—or found some way to steal that watch.

FIVE

Jordan and Uriah followed Master Henning down a dirt path behind the big house. It was getting dark and the man carried a lantern that lit small patches of the trees and outbuildings. Jordan was glad that he didn't have to spend the night alone in the swamp woods, but he worried that this place would be even worse. He didn't like what he'd seen of it so far. He eyed the broad silhouette of the master's back. If the master carried the watch in a back pocket, getting it would be easy, but no way could he go around in front of him and take it from his vest.

While Jordan thought about the watch, Uriah pointed out the different outbuildings: the kitchen, the chicken coop, the smokehouse, the barn, the stables and carriage house, the spinning and weaving hut, and the overseer's office. Jordan had to admit that this was an awesome farm, but he wanted no part of being a slave on it.

In the distance Jordan heard people singing, talking, and laughing, and he smelled smoke. He and Uriah soon came to a cluster of tiny log shacks, huddled together. There must have been a dozen. In front of every cabin somebody leaned or squatted against an open door as if on guard. When they stood and said "Evenin', Masta," everybody inside hushed.

Jordan and Uriah followed the master into a shack on the left. It had only one tiny room and was swarming with people. Two grown-ups, who Jordan guessed must be Uriah's parents, one old man, and five children. Right away Jordan noticed that Uriah's skin color was lighter than the others'. More like his own. He thought the youngest kid must have been about three years old, and the oldest around fourteen. The fireplace on one wall looked like it had been made out of dried mud; it puffed so much smoke that Jordan had a hard time breathing. The mom knelt by it, cooking something in a black iron skillet that smelled like stale bacon. Because there weren't any windows the room was hot as hell and full of smoke. There wasn't even a real floor. Just hard-packed dirt.

When they saw the master, everybody in the room except the littlest kid stopped laughing and talking and stood up.

"Evenin', Masta," they said. Jordan wondered where he was supposed to sleep. He didn't see any beds. Just a pile of old worn-out blankets shoved into a corner. There didn't seem to be enough room for all these people to lie down. No chairs either; when he came in, everyone had been sitting on the floor. He was shocked to see that people actually lived like this. It was hardly any different from the animal pens they had just seen.

The master tried to explain what Jordan was doing there, but he finally gave up and told Uriah's parents that Jordan would be staying in their cabin until he could locate his owner. Jordan gritted his teeth. Owner! That's what he thinks! No way! As soon as everyone was asleep, he was going to sneak into the big house and get that watch. Then he was blowing this place for good.

When the master left, the whole family stood around Jordan and stared as if he were some alien from outer space. The kids felt his Levi's and Nikes, and asked where he got them. Jordan tried to explain about stores and shopping malls, but he could tell that they didn't believe him. Even as upset and scared as he was, he couldn't help enjoying their oohs and aahs and admiring looks.

At suppertime Uriah's mom gave everybody one little fried corn cake and a tiny scrap of something called salt pork. The grown-ups and Jordan got theirs on tin plates. There was no table; everybody just sat on the dirt floor to eat. And they all ate with their fingers because there weren't any forks or spoons. The kids held their corn cakes with dirty hands, grease running down their chins and arms.

All during the meal, they swatted and brushed away the flies buzzing around them. It didn't take Jordan long to finish that little corn cake and that tiny scrap of meat. He was still hungry and thought about the pizza Mom and Tachelle were probably having at that very minute. He could just see those cheese strings pull the way they do when he lifted a piece out of the box. His mouth watered.

He hoped Uriah's mom would make them another batch of corn cakes, or give them something else, but she didn't. She poured the grease out of the skillet into a cracked bowl and set it to one side of the fireplace. Jordan noticed that she hadn't eaten. Then she sat down by Uriah's daddy and ate the half of his cake he'd saved for her. Jordan realized then that he'd eaten the food meant for her, and she'd never said a word about it. There was something about her that reminded him of Mom. It was her eyes. The very same eyes. Big and black and tilted up a little at the corners. She was related to Mom, no question about it.

After they finished eating, and when the light in the fireplace grew dim, Uriah's mom lit a piece of string floating in a little pan of grease. It made a faint light that threw big shadows on the walls. Then everybody sat in front of Jordan and stared. In spite of the worries that haunted him, he decided to relax for a few minutes and enjoy being the evening's star attraction. It would be fun to amaze these poor slaves.

"In my time," he said, "which is way off in the future for you guys, we have what we call electricity. Like right here, tonight, if you had electricity, you could just flip a little switch on the wall, and a little glass bulb in the ceiling would make it light as day in here. You could just throw out that little pan of grease with the string in it."

One of Uriah's sisters, a skinny little thing with big eyes, asked, "Did you bring some of that electricity to show us?"

Jordan laughed while the others just stared at him. "I'd be dead, little girl, dead! Electrocuted if I tried to carry electricity around with me—and you'd be fried too if you touched me. But just because I can't take it with me and show it to you doesn't mean it's not real." He thought he'd answered her pretty well, but then Uriah's daddy fired a question at him.

"In your time, as you say, just where does this electricity come from?"

Jordan was surprised to realize that he had no idea how to answer that question. For once he was actually sorry that he'd skipped school. He should have gone that day when Mr. Clifton talked about electric power and the environment. "It's in the walls," Jordan said. "We have little holes in the walls, and everything you want to work or run, you just plug into the holes." He knew he probably hadn't given the answer Uriah's dad wanted, but it was the best he could do.

"And we have television," Jordan said. "Everybody has one of these boxes in their houses. It has a glass screen on one side of it. You plug it into the electricity and turn a knob or press a button, and you can see colored pictures of people talking and singing and telling the news from all over the world."

"Can you hear 'em too?" asked Uriah.

"You bet you can."

"I don't believe it," said Uriah's oldest brother.

"It's true."

"Prove it."

"I can't. Because you don't have any electricity or equipment." It surprised Jordan that these slaves didn't seem more impressed with his world. And when he told them about cars, airplanes, telephones, and computers, they wanted to know more about them than he knew. They asked about the inventions that led up to them, how voices came through wires, and how little tiny chips smaller than your fingernail could carry mountains of information. Jordan couldn't answer any of their questions. They seemed to think that if he couldn't explain how these things worked, he must be making it all up. They may be uneducated slaves, Jordan thought, but he had to admit they weren't dumb.

The oldest boy, whose name was Rabe, did nothing for Jordan's ego when he looked at the others and said, "He done gone crazy. If he don't watch out, he be ready for one of them loony 'sylums."

"Rabe!" cried his mom, "that's no way to treat our guest! Tell him you're sorry."

He hung his head and picked at his toes. "I'm sorry," he mumbled.

"Aw, forget it." Jordan looked up at Uriah's mom. She seemed like a nice lady, and after all that talking he was hungrier than ever. His stomach felt hollow. "Is there anything more to eat?"

"No," the mother said in a kindly voice. "Our food's runnin' low, and issue day ain't until the end of the month."

"Issue day? What's that?" Jordan asked.

Uriah and all his brothers and sisters giggled. One of his little sisters pointed to Jordan and said, "He don't know what issue day is!"

Jordan felt that she was doing her best to make

him look foolish. "Okay, I never heard of it," he said. "So what?"

"Son," said Uriah's father, "on issue day we gets our supplies. Every month or so the masta, he send a wagon to the quarters with our cornmeal and pickled pork, and every family get two bushel of cornmeal and eight pound of meat."

"Nothing else?" Jordan asked.

"That be all the masta give us, but we raises a few vegetables in our garden in summer. And sometimes we catches a fish or two, or hunts a possum. So we don't starve."

Jordan was amazed. How could people who lived on a farm have so little to eat? He slapped a mosquito that bit his arm. Another one was whining at his ear. It seemed to him that the bugs owned the place.

Jordan went with the others to the stinky outhouse at the end of the cabin row. He sneaked around behind it and peed where the smell wasn't so bad.

Back at the cabin, Uriah's mom handed out blankets. There weren't enough to go around, so she told Jordan to sleep on Uriah's blanket. He followed Uriah to where all the other males in the cabin were getting ready to lie down. The boys and men spread out their blankets on one side of the cabin, the girls on the other. The parents slept together, their heads to the wall separating the two sides.

"There's more room on the other side," Jordan said to Uriah. "Why can't we sleep there?"

"That's the girls' side. My mama and papa, they's strict about sleepin' places. We has to sleep right here." He spread his blanket out between Rabe and his grandpa. Jordan was hoping to lie down next to the door so that he could sneak out while the others slept. He absolutely had to get into the big house and steal the watch. He hoped that just holding that watch in his hand might be enough to send him back to the street underpass.

Before they all lay down, Uriah took one of Jordan's hands and Rabe took the other and the whole family formed a big circle. Uriah's dad, a dark-skinned man called Seth, said a prayer. "Lord, bless this family and our visitor too, wherever he be from. And tomorrow, be with us in our toil and suffering. Guide us to do right, so's not to anger the overseer. And Lord, we know that one day you'll show us all the way to freedom."

That man's voice, both proud and humble, moved Jordan nearly to tears, but he managed to swallow the lump in his throat. Then Uriah's mom went around to all of them, Jordan too. She gave each of them a hug and said, "The Lord bless and keep you." To Jordan's embarrassment, he felt a tear slide down his cheek. He sure wasn't acting the way a Cobra should. He realized how homesick he was for Mom and Tachelle. Uriah's mom reminded him so much of his own mother. And he was struck by how they all took him in as if he were one of their own.

After good-nights, they all lay down on their blankets. Jordan couldn't help noticing that nobody brushed their teeth, washed, or bathed. After all, how could they? Their water came from a well, a bucketful at a time. They didn't even change clothes. The others were all barefoot anyway, so Jordan was the only one who took his shoes off.

Jordan was just settling down when Uriah whispered, "I believes what you said 'bout 'lectricity and all them things you tol' us. While you was talkin', I kept thinkin' maybe there be boxes of time stacked on top o' each other. Maybe they was a hole in the one you was in and you just slid through it."

"Yeah! Maybe that is sort of how it happened."
Jordan was so relieved that someone actually be-
lieved him. And Uriah had imagination, all right.
Boxes of time! Jordan couldn't help smiling.

"I is glad you slipped through that hole," Uriah
said. Since Jordan was stuck here, at least for the
next hour or two, he felt better knowing that not
everyone thought he was crazy.

Though it was now pitch-dark outside, it was
hot as fire in the cabin. The flies and mosquitoes
were all over Jordan. Slapping them away kept
him pretty busy.

"They ain't nothin' to fret 'bout," Uriah whispered. "The snakes that crawls in, now they's
somethin' to steal your sleep."

His words made Jordan's flesh crawl. He hated
snakes. "How often does that happen?"

"I reckon whenever they've a mind to."

Jordan wanted to know the odds. "How many
snakes, in a year's time?"

"Year's time? I don't know what you is talkin'
about. We got plantin' time, we got hoein' time, we
got pickin' time. We got Christmas too, then we goes
from Sunday to Sunday. Which one you mean?"

"Okay, from Sunday to Sunday then, how many
snakes come into the cabin?"

"Sometimes none. Sometimes one or two. Dependin' on whether it's plantin' or pickin' time."

Jordan remembered Uriah's saying it was picking time. "Picking time, then. How many snakes?"

"Mostly none."

That word "mostly" bothered Jordan. Oh, well, he wasn't going to be staying here but an hour or two anyway, and he figured that he could beat the odds.

Soon the sound of heavy breathing filled the cabin. Jordan decided to wait a few more minutes, just to be sure that every last person was asleep before he took off for the big house.

SIX

In the dark, Jordan stumbled
past the outbuildings and crept toward the back
door of the big house. Then all of a sudden the
dogs tied out back growled and went into a bark-
ing frenzy. When Jordan heard a woman's voice
yell "Who's there?" he spun around and didn't
stop running until he reached the quarters.

When he entered the cabin and lay down beside
Uriah he was shaking from head to foot. Man,
that was a close call. He'd forgotten about the
dogs. Luckily everyone here was still asleep. He
decided to rest awhile and go back later, only next
time he'd try the front door.

It was still dark when Uriah shook Jordan's
shoulder. "Get up," he said. "Overseer's blowin'

the conker shell." Jordan couldn't believe that he'd slept through the night. Mad at himself, he realized he had no choice now. He'd have to go back to the big house this morning and look for the watch in the master's bedroom. It might be better anyway, because he'd be able to see what he was doing. He hoped that it wasn't something the master wore every day. All of a sudden he heard a loud, mournful sound. Curious, Jordan went to the door. Through the gray light before sunrise he saw a tall white guy in a big straw hat and a musclebound black man walking between the cabins. The black one was blowing on something that looked like a big seashell.

"The white man be the overseer," Uriah explained. "We calls him Mista Travis, and the nigger be his helper. We calls him the driver. Name's Buster." Mr. Travis saw Jordan and walked over to him.

Jordan ducked inside, but there wasn't any place to hide. The overseer stuck his head in the door.

"You! Come here," he said to Jordan. "The master tol' me we'd have a new picker today. You must be the one."

"You got it all wrong, mister," Jordan said. "I'm not a slave. You see, I'm here by accident. I don't even belong in this century. Where I come from, everybody's free."

The overseer shook his head. "I've heard some smart-mouthed niggers in my day, but you take the prize, boy." He walked into the cabin and grabbed the back of Jordan's shirt collar. A wave of fear welled up from Jordan's toes and rose to his throat. He knew he was no match for the beefy overseer, so he didn't put up a fight. He'd have to think his way out of this instead. Everybody in the cabin froze and watched.

"I'll tell ya right now, boy," said the man, "if you try any more back talk, you'll get stripes on your back you won't forget, and you'll wish you ain't never been born in any century. You hear me, don't you, boy?"

Jordan swallowed the urge to answer and just nodded. As soon as possible he'd run and hide in the woods, then sneak into the big house and grab the watch.

Mr. Travis turned to Uriah's dad. "What you think of this here boy?"

"He seem a little moonstruck, sir," said Seth. "Otherwise he be all right."

The overseer tightened his grip on Jordan's shirt collar and pulled him out the door. "You

stay with me, boy. We got business to attend to."
Mr. Travis pulled him over to the driver. Jordan
started unbuttoning his shirt, thinking he could
duck out of it and run, but the driver saw what
he was doing and slipped a loop of scratchy rope
over his head and around his neck. He and the
overseer led Jordan, by the rope, some fifty yards
or so behind a toolshed to a thick post set in the
ground. It must have been eight feet tall.

"In case you never seen nothin' like this in that
'other life' you was yappin' about, this is our
whippin' post." The overseer held Jordan while
the black man took the rope off his neck and tied
it around his wrists and lashed them to the post,
above his head. Jordan gasped and saw spots in
front of his eyes. Stay cool, he kept telling himself.
This can't be happening! The braided leather whip
the overseer took out of his back pocket uncoiled
like a snake. He handed it to the driver, who
swung a couple of practice lashes on the side of
the shed. Jordan's heart pounded.

"Hear that?" asked the overseer. Jordan nodded.
If they were going to do it, then just do it and get
it over with! He thought of the welts on Uriah's
back, and of the beautiful big perch he and his dad
had caught once. It flopped and wiggled on the

line until it worked itself free. Maybe he could do the same.

The overseer took the whip, coiled it back up, and stuck it in his pocket. "If we wasn't so short-handed we woulda given you ten lashes. Ain't no sense in hobblin' an extra hand, but remember this place when you've a mind to talk outta turn." While he was still tied to the post, the overseer took Jordan's shoes off and handed them to the driver.

"Here, Buster, try these on. They look too little for me." Jordan kept his mouth shut, but inside he was screaming, My Nikes! Not my Nikes!

Buster put them on and did a little dance. "Whoeeee! Them's a little tight but they be mighty fancy! Mighty fancy!" Then the two of them took off Jordan's shirt.

"This oughta fit my oldest boy," said the overseer. Jordan's jeans went next, then his briefs. He was standing there stark naked, wondering what next, when Buster went into the shed and brought out a burlap shirt like Uriah's.

"This here oughta be about right," he said. A prison uniform, Jordan thought, but he didn't dare say anything. The two men untied his hands and held him while he put it on. The coarse cloth itched. Then they put the rope leash on him again and marched him back to the quarters where the slaves had lined up in front of the cabins. There must have been fifty or sixty of them.

The driver took off Jordan's rope and put him between Uriah and Rabe. "That your place, boy," he said. "Don't you forget where you belongs." Belong? No way, man! Jordan thought. Then the overseer asked about a slave who was missing.

"Where's Thaddeus?"

"Sir," said a woman with a blue bandanna tied around her head, "he got the fever bad."

"He was workin' yesterday," said the overseer.

"He be workin' sir, but he feel bad all day, and last night he had the misery with the fever and the shakes. He ain't fittin' fo' work, sir."

"Well, we'll see about that." The overseer went into the cabin to check on Thaddeus. Jordan thought about playing sick, but if he did it right now, it would look like he'd gotten the idea from Thaddeus. Maybe he'd try it later.

Jordan, so hungry that he could have eaten a bear, wondered if he'd missed breakfast. Uriah's mom was carrying a greasy cloth bundle; Jordan hoped it held something to eat. While the slaves waited for the overseer to come out of Thaddeus's cabin, Buster handed each of them a heavy roll of coarse cloth.

"What's this?" Jordan asked Uriah.

"Cotton sack," he said. Jordan started to unroll it.

"Don't do that now," Uriah said. "It be too big. Won't be time to roll it back up 'fore we walks to the field."

Mr. Travis came out of the cabin shaking his head, and said, "Thaddeus won't be comin', so the rest of you will have to work extra hard to take up the slack."

With the overseer at the head of the line, and the driver behind them, Jordan marched with the others, in twos, to the field. The slaves sang. Uriah whispered to Jordan that the songs were about freedom, but the overseer either didn't listen to the words or didn't care. Once in a while Mr. Travis cracked his whip on the ground. Jordan decided it was just to scare them.

As far as Jordan could see, the land was dotted white with cotton plants in bloom. It was a pretty sight, like nothing he'd ever seen before; the balls of white cotton bursting out all over the tall plants looked like tufts of fluffy snow. The plants had zillions of branches and some were as tall as the grown-ups' waists. Buster, the driver, came up to Jordan and told him that he would be working on the same row with Uriah's mom. He called her Clara.

"You pick this side and Clara, she pick the other," he said. "And you best keep up, 'cause she be one of the fast pickers. If you lags behind, you gets the whip, so you best make your fingers fly." He studied Jordan as he unrolled the cotton bag. Jordan stared at it in disbelief. It must have been ten feet long and had a strap loop on one end. He saw that Clara had slipped the strap over her head and across her shoulder, so he did the same. The bag opened at his side, just above his waist; on Clara it opened chest high.

"You ever pick cotton before?" asked the driver.

"No, sir."

"I didn't think so." Then he said, "We gonna be watchin' you, boy, so you best catch on quick if you don't want a right smart whippin'." He nodded to Uriah's mom. "Clara, you tell him what he need to know." He walked back to where the overseer stood.

The slaves near Jordan were going after the cotton with both hands and slipping it into their bags with lightning speed. To Jordan, it didn't look that hard.

"Now, Jordan," Clara said, "let me see you pull the cotton outta that pod there. We calls it the boll." Jordan sighed the way he always did when Mom preached at him. What did she think he was? Some kind of an idiot? He'd show her that any dummy could pick cotton. He grabbed at a cotton bloom and yanked at it. The boll holding the cotton came off. So did a branch with unopened bolls.

"Lord a'mighty! What you think you doin'?" she whispered. "If Buster or the overseer caught you doin' that, you'd get the whip for sure."

"Just for that?"

"You pull off the boll with the cotton and a branch full of bolls that ain't opened yet." In one easy snatch she plucked the cotton out of the boll and put it in Jordan's sack. Then she stooped down and buried the boll and broken branch in the loose dirt by their dusty bare feet.

"What are you doing that for?" Jordan asked.

"We can't let Buster and Mr. Travis see what you done tore off." She nodded at the two huge wicker baskets at the start of the row. "The one on that side's mine and the one on this side's yours. When your sack is full, you empty it in your basket. The overseer, he weigh it at sundown, and if it

don't weigh heavy enough you gets a whippin'."
Jordan didn't believe they'd go that far. This stuff
was light as air. Well, he was onto that old "scare
the new kid" trick. This was probably just like
what the overseer was doing when he and Buster
slapped that whip in front of him and didn't end
up using it. Yeah, they probably made her tell him
that. But then he couldn't quite chase away the
memory of Uriah's scars.

"You hurry along, now, boy," Clara said, " 'cause
we got to do this whole row before nightfall."

Jordan squinted into the distance, but couldn't
make out the end. Just tons of cotton fading out
of sight.

"You better get busy, boy, 'cause that's all a
good hand can do in a day."

Jordan pulled at the fluffy white stuff, and often
as not the boll came off in his hand. He seldom
bothered to take the cotton out and just tossed the
whole thing in his bag. They probably had a way
of cleaning it, so what difference could it make?
Besides, the bolls would make the cotton weigh
more. He noticed that the bag hanging from
his neck kept swinging from side to side when he
walked, leaving a trail of broken low branches. He
tried to keep an eye out for some way to skip out

and steal the watch, but whenever he looked up, Buster was right nearby, staring at him.

The sun rose higher, and soon he was boiling hot. Sweat ran down his forehead into his eyes. His empty stomach growled and he was so thirsty that he would have given his right arm for a cold bottle of Coke.

"Do you have anything to drink?" he called out to Clara. She was several yards ahead of him by now, plucking the white stuff with both hands and tossing it into her bag. She looked up but never stopped working. He could see that her bag was filling up while his own was still nearly empty.

"The water boy be comin' soon," she said.

He worked on and on in the boiling heat. A little later a small boy who couldn't have been older than six or seven walked toward him, half dragging a heavy bucket.

"You needs a drink?" he asked. So this was the water boy.

Jordan hesitated to drink from the dipper he offered. How many mouths had touched that thing? But his thirst quickly overcame his disgust and he drank eagerly. The water was warm and not very refreshing, but at least it was wet.

He was monstrously hungry and it wasn't long

before he was thirsty again too. Would the water boy come back? He was nowhere to be seen. Jordan felt dizzy from the heat. He didn't realize what was happening when he saw dark spots in front of his eyes. Then everything went black. The next thing Jordan knew he was lying in the dirt, and the overseer was standing over him whacking him with the whip. At first he was too surprised to feel the pain.

"What you doin', boy, layin' down on the job?"

"I must have passed out," he said.

"We don't have time for faintin' around here, boy. You better get up and go at it if you know what's good for you." When Jordan got up on his knees, the whip cracked across his back again. Jordan gasped at its fiery sting.

"Up, boy! All the way up! And I wanta see that basket full by nightfall or you're gonna be mighty sorry." As Jordan staggered to his feet, the overseer opened the boy's bag and looked inside. "Whatta you mean, boy, throwin' the bolls in with the cotton! And you broke branches! Don't you know that broke branches is dead branches? And dead branches don't give no cotton!" For that, Travis gave him another lash.

By that time Jordan was crazy with pain. Blood ran down his legs and he was so angry that he wanted to grab the whip and make that overseer feel even worse than *he* did, but he didn't dare. The man would probably kill him. There *had* to be laws against this kind of treatment.

"I'm gonna tell the police on you!" he blurted out.

"Ha ha ha!" Travis laughed. "You ain't gonna get nowhere with our sheriff, boy. He don't like lazy niggers and would just as soon shoot you as not."

Jordan hated that man. How dare *he* call him that! Pain fired his rage. He stared at Travis and Travis stared back, then walked off. Angry as he was, there wasn't a thing Jordan could do then but just go on picking cotton. He knew that if he ran for the big house he'd be caught—and worse.

SEVEN

Hot, sore, thirsty, and bleeding, Jordan couldn't believe he was still alive after that endless morning in the cotton field. Clara had done all she could to help him. When the driver and the overseer weren't watching, Clara had come over to his side of the row, picked his cotton, and put it in his sack. Jordan now knew that they meant business when they said not to put the bolls in with the cotton, and not to break the branches. But he was slow. There was more to picking cotton than he'd figured. Once, when the water boy came by again, Clara had moistened a rag and tied it around Jordan's head to cool him. It helped.

At noon the driver blew the conker shell, and the families got together in the field to eat. Uriah's mom untied that greasy bag she wore around her waist and gave Jordan and each member of her family one corn cake and a tiny piece of fried salt pork. If they hadn't shared with him, Jordan was sure he would have died of hunger. During the meal, Uriah and his brothers and sisters joked and told riddles, none of which Jordan understood. But they smiled at him and treated him like one of the family.

After about ten minutes Buster blew the conker shell again and everybody got up and went back to work. Uriah had told the truth. Lunch was just a corn cake eaten on the run.

Amazingly, the afternoon was harder than the morning because it was hotter. Jordan's whipped back hurt. So did his shoulders and arms and his fingers, which were pricked raw from the cotton plants. Whenever he saw spots in front of his eyes, he put his head down the way Uriah's mom had told him to. He didn't dare pass out again. The cotton field was an endless hell. Clara was so far ahead of him that she looked like a dot amid the shimmering heat waves. When she dragged her heavy sack to the basket, she'd stop to see how Jordan was doing. When the overseer and driver weren't looking, she'd stuff some of her cotton into his sack. Then she'd rub his head with a damp cloth and give him a hug. To Jordan, she was a life-saver.

Even after the sun went down, Jordan and the others worked on and on until it was too dark to see. Then, when they heard the conker shell announce quitting time, they dragged their sacks to the baskets for one last dumping. Jordan's muscles ached from the day's work, his whipped back stung with every move, and his fingers bled. Even worse, his basket was half empty. He knew it would be too light, and braced himself for another whipping. Uriah's mom had trouble dragging her basket, so Jordan helped her move it along. No more of this. Jordan would get that watch tonight and say good-bye to this place forever!

Clara and Jordan followed the others to a building at the edge of the field. Light from a lantern flickered in the doorway. Frogs croaked and crickets chirped. The slaves, dragging their baskets, formed a line outside. Jordan trembled and wanted to run, but it was dark and the only hiding place around here was the woods. At night, even Uriah's cabin seemed safer.

Mr. Travis hung Clara's basket onto his scale. He seemed surprised, as if he couldn't believe what he saw, and weighed it again. "You're short," he told her. "Six pounds short." He pulled her over to one side where two other slaves stood with their wrists tied. Jordan guessed that they were waiting to be whipped. Buster tied a rope around Clara's wrists too. Jordan felt miserable. He couldn't just stand there and let her be punished. She was short because she'd helped him. He'd probably be whipped for opening his mouth, but he was bound to get it anyway for short weight.

"It's not her fault," Jordan told Travis. "Her basket was short because she was busy teaching me."

The overseer hooked Jordan's basket on the scale, then glared at him with icy blue eyes. The lamp hanging on the hook above his head threw a yellow beam on his long bony face. "Who asked you?"

Jordan knew there was no safe way to answer that question, and said nothing. But Travis continued to stare at Jordan and asked again. "Well, answer me, boy. Who asked you?"

Jordan lifted his chin and stared right back at him. "Nobody. That's why I'm telling you."

"You gotta be taught to hold that uppity tongue, boy." He weighed Jordan's basket. "You ain't pullin' your weight. If she was teachin' you to pick, she wasn't doin' a good job." The overseer glanced at Buster, who stood beside him. "Take him out to the post, Buster. Ten lashes, and don't go shortin' on him, 'cause I'll be countin' every one. This lazy nigger's gotta learn some respect and how to work."

Ten lashes! Jordan wondered how he would live through it. The three he'd had in the field still burned. The blood had dried up but his wounds would be torn open. What if they got infected? There wouldn't be any medicines here to save his life. When Buster grabbed him by the arm and led him out into the night, Jordan thought he was probably going to die. Die. Trapped in this nightmarish time warp.

When Buster tied his wrists to the post, Jordan thought about Mom, Tachelle, and Daddy. Grandpa too. They'd never know what had happened to him. He was sure that he'd never see them again, ever. King and the other homeboys popped in and out of his thoughts but they didn't stick the way his family did. One thing, if he did die from this, he wouldn't get beat up for not making the meeting at Baker's parking lot. What a weird thought! He needed a prayer and tried to remember the ones he'd learned when he was little and went to Sunday school, but his mind was racing too fast. The only words that came to him were *God help me.*

Jordan listened to the crickets and frogs and heard Buster stirring around several feet away. It was so dark that he couldn't see much. What was taking him so long? He wanted to get it over with! He was bracing himself for the first lash when all of a sudden Buster whispered in his ear.

"I gonna crack the whip on the ground, and every time you hears it, you scream loud as you can. Then after four or five lashes you go dead quiet. They all faints after four or five." Buster was going to fake it. Relief surged through Jordan.

"Why are you doing this for me?" he asked.

"We coloreds gotta stick together. You just lucky Mr. Travis ain't watchin', and if you says one word 'bout this to any livin' soul, you gonna get the real thing. From me." Jordan realized then how big a risk this man was taking for him.

"What if he finds out?"

"If he don't kill me, I reckon I be sold to the trader."

"Would he really kill you?"

"It happen mor'n once 'round here."

"But that's murder!" Jordan whispered.

"Killin' a nigger don't count for murder. The law don't protect no coloreds." The unfairness of it made Jordan so furious that he wanted to yell even before Buster cracked the whip.

"You ready?" Buster asked.

"Yeah," Jordan said. "And thanks."

When Buster finished the fake beating, Jordan realized that his acting job wasn't over. He had to pretend to be in pain, but he couldn't let anyone see his back. So he staggered into the hut moaning and groaning. Uriah spread his blanket out for Jordan, who sat on it, his back just a few inches from the wall. Uriah, his dad Seth, and the other kids stood around him, trying to comfort him. Jordan noticed that Uriah's mom hadn't come in yet. He hoped Buster would fake it for her too. But what if Travis watched, or did the beating himself? Jordan yelled when Seth pulled off his shirt. He hoped Seth wouldn't notice that his shirt had only dried blood on it. If he did, he asked no questions. Jordan pulled his back just a little farther away from the wall when Seth poured a strong-smelling liquid on it. The stuff hurt like the devil and he couldn't help moaning.

"What is that?" Jordan asked.

"Turpentine," Seth said. "Nothing better for open sores." Then Jordan heard screaming in the distance. Was it real or fake? For Buster's sake, Jordan hoped his own had sounded that real.

A little later Uriah's mom staggered into the hut breathing heavily, then she collapsed in the doorway. The blood from her stripes showed through her burlap clothes. The rest of the family helped her onto her blanket. Uriah's dad went out to borrow more turpentine while Rabe brewed her some rotten-smelling herb tea. Clara's hurt was real. Her groans sent Jordan on a real guilt trip. So that's what she got for helping him through the worst day of his life. It was no use trying to hold back his tears.

Rabe must have thought Jordan's sobs came from the whipping, because he made him a cup of that awful tea. Jordan thanked him but begged off, saying that he felt too sick to drink it.

He was so exhausted that he gave up all thoughts of sneaking into the big house that night. He'd get some sleep, then in the morning pretend to be sicker than he was and get excused from work. Then, one way or another, nothing, not even the risk of the whip, would stop him from getting inside that mansion—and getting his hands on that watch.

EIGHT

The next morning Jordan didn't get up when Buster blew the conker shell. He didn't even have to pretend he was sick. His back burned from the whipping and his muscles ached so much he could hardly move. Next to him, Uriah moaned and shook.

"What's wrong?" Jordan asked.

"I gots the shakes and fever again," he said.

"Have you had it before?"

"I gets it 'bout once a week."

"Is it catching?" Jordan was in enough trouble without getting some disease.

"I dunno." Uriah's teeth chattered. "Lotsa peoples has it, even the white folks in the big house."

Jordan was surprised to hear that. Seth came over to see Uriah and gave him some of that tea left over from the night before. Uriah drank it down. The cure-all, Jordan thought scornfully. Great for whippings, fever, and chills, and probably snakebite too. It was hard for him to believe that people around here actually survived at all. Well, this was positively his last day. He was going to get the watch and be zapped back to the real world.

Clara, when she heard Uriah was sick, stumbled over to him and put a wet cloth on his forehead. She looked so weak herself that she could barely stand up. Then she asked Jordan how he was feeling. He moaned and pretended to be sicker than he was. Any minute now the overseer would be coming in to check on him, and he had to practice. She stood over Jordan and pressed his forehead with the same damp cloth she'd used on Uriah. Jordan didn't want to hurt her feelings by telling her not to do that. After all, what could she possibly know about the way germs travel from one person to another?

The three of them, Uriah, his mom, and Jordan, stayed on their blankets while the others went out to line up. Jordan wasn't sure what he'd do if

Travis asked to see his back and was relieved when Buster came instead. Buster probably asked for the job to save his own skin, and Travis let him do it because he trusted him. This sure was one messed-up place, full of lies and fear.

"How you feelin' this mornin'?" Buster asked Jordan.

"Not so good," he said.

"You able to stand up? If you able to stand, you able to work."

"No, sir."

He didn't ask Jordan any more questions, then went over to quiz Uriah and his mom. He excused them all from work and left. Outside, the horn blew and the singing faded as the workers marched off to the fields. Jordan waited till he couldn't hear them anymore, then got up and looked out the door. When they marched out of sight, he tiptoed back to where Uriah was curled up on his blanket. He'd stopped shaking, but his eyes were closed. Clara slept too. Jordan took off for the big house.

He peeked over a spicy-smelling bush and studied the backyard. Tree shadows spread across the huge white house. Even this early in the morning the air was hot and still. The house slaves hurried in and out the back door. The dogs sat on the grass, which was still damp with dew. They panted and watched, alert to every sound. No way would Jordan be able to get through that back door without being seen or barked at. He'd have to try the other side of the house.

There was no one on the wide front porch. Jordan climbed the steps and stopped. Through a big open window he heard voices and the clink and clatter of dishes. The master and his family must be having breakfast. Jordan slowly opened the massive front door and stepped inside a huge hall where a graceful wooden staircase curved up to the second floor. From where Jordan stood, he could see into the dining room. The master sat at the head of a long table with his family, his back to Jordan. He had on a fancy bathrobe with gray satin stripes. Jordan figured that if he was still in his bathrobe he probably wouldn't be wearing his watch. Maybe it would still be on his dresser or in a drawer. Jordan felt his stomach flutter with fear and excitement. The master's bedroom was probably upstairs. It would without a doubt be the biggest and the best of all the rooms.

Jordan tiptoed up that grand, shiny staircase, careful to stay on a strip of carpet running up the middle so as not to make a sound. He'd never been in such a big house before. It seemed more like a ritzy hotel or the art museums he'd been to on field trips. He wanted to stop and stare at the paintings on the walls, each one in a fancy gold frame. Talk about rich! The house was a world apart from the slaves' cabins. But he had to keep his mind on what he was doing and not waste any time.

In the hall upstairs he peeked into a bedroom where a young slave girl in a long skirt and apron was making a bed. She was working so hard that she didn't even notice when Jordan darted past the open door. Next he stepped into a bedroom that just had to be the master's. It was super-deluxe and stretched all the way across the front of the house. Jordan was relieved to see that the bed was already made.

Quickly scanning the tops of three polished dressers, Jordan saw candlesticks, carved wooden boxes, tiny portraits in silver frames, and a silver comb, brush, and mirror—but no watch. He constantly looked over his shoulder, afraid of being discovered. His fingers shook as he opened the wooden boxes, one after another. Just buttons and coins. Then, slowly, he opened the top drawer of a dresser, praying that it wouldn't squeak. Whew! But there was nothing in there except shirts.

He had just begun to open the top drawer of another chest when he heard voices in the upstairs hall. It was the master and his wife—and they were headed his way! Jordan's heart rose into his throat. Hide! he told himself. Now! He dropped onto his stomach and slid under the long ruffled bed skirt. Not a second too soon. The footsteps in the room became louder and louder, and then stopped. Jordan could tell they were no more than a few feet away.

"Please shut the door, John. I don't want the servants to hear. They gossip so."

As soon as the door had closed, the mistress said, "I happen to know, John, that you are not paying our bills as promptly as they ought to be paid. Yesterday Mr. McIntire refused to show me the new cloth from his London shipment. When I asked him why, he told me that you hadn't settled our account there for several months. I declare, it was too humiliating for words—and I want an explanation!"

"Well, Lavinia my dear, our income may be a

little short until the whole cotton crop comes in, but there will soon be enough money for anything your heart desires."

"When can you pay Mr. McIntire?"

"Not for a while, dear, but I'll talk to him. I'm sure he'll understand."

Jordan huddled under the bed, finding it hard to believe that anybody living in a house like this could ever be short of money.

"John," said Lavinia, "I find I am forced to speak to you frankly. Your spendthrift ways are the talk of the county. Changes will have to be made, but in the meantime, we'll just have to raise some money."

"And how does my little sweet propose to do that?"

"The same way we've done it in the past."

"Now, Lavinia, I would rather not sell any more slaves. As it is, we're down to a bare minimum for a plantation of this size."

Jordan's mouth fell open, but he had to keep his feelings under control. Keep quiet, he told himself. Try not to breathe too hard.

"Would you rather sell our paintings? Our furniture? Our silver?"

"Lavinia! Don't be ridiculous! Think of the

humiliation! We'd never be able to face our neighbors!"

"Then what about a few acres of land?"

"Never! Land is our most precious possession."

"Well, Mr. Andrews has had his eye on Black Prince for some time. He once offered you three hundred dollars."

"Now, Lavinia, that's not fair. I love that horse."

They didn't say anything more for a while. Jordan heard them walking around opening drawers. When he peered through the lace on the bed ruffle, he saw the master standing behind his wife, pulling strings on some kind of underwear that pinched her in the middle.

"Tighter," she said. "There. That's about right."

Jordan kept watching, hoping to see which drawer the master took the watch from. The man put on his vest and tugged at it, trying to smooth it over his fat belly. Then he reached for the top drawer of the chest that Jordan had just started to search. Seeing that it was still slightly open, the master paused and a puzzled frown creased his face. Then he took the watch out, wound it, and placed it in his vest pocket. Damn! Jordan thought. If only I'd opened that drawer first!

"I hear slaves are bringing a good price these days," said the mistress.

The master sank into a chair. "I suppose you're right, Lavinia. No one would think anything of our selling a few slaves. After all, even the most respectable landowners do that occasionally." Jordan couldn't understand how anyone could possibly think that selling people was more respectable than selling furniture or paintings. Then he had a strange thought. Back in his own time he might have liked the master. His manner and personality reminded him of the doctor he and Mom and Tachelle went to. A nice, gentle guy. But for all that, owning slaves had turned the master into something evil! Jordan wanted to rush out and make the man understand this, but he was afraid the master might have him killed. Until he got that watch and found the underpass, he was trapped. Jordan shook with rage as he pulled his head farther back under the bed.

"I hear the trader will be in town soon," the master went on. "If we decide now, we'll be ready for him. You understand, don't you, Lavinia, that you can't breathe a word about this. If we don't take the slaves by surprise, they're sure to try and run away."

"Yes, and it's always so unpleasant to send the hounds after them."

The hounds? Jordan had seen movies where dogs hunted down criminals. Unpleasant, she says! Yeah, sure, she'd be holed up here in this mansion and wouldn't have to watch scared black guys being chewed up and ripped to pieces.

"Would you consider parting with any of your household help, Lavinia?"

"How could I, John? We have three big parties coming up this fall, and my mother and sister and her family are coming to stay for several weeks. I couldn't possibly spare a one."

Jordan ground his teeth. Poor woman might have to soil her lily-white hands with cooking and cleaning and dishwashing. Visions of Clara—and his own mom—swam through his mind.

The master sighed. "Well, then, I suppose we must sell a few field hands. Mr. Travis is going to be pretty unhappy, now that picking time is upon us."

"What do you care what Mr. Travis thinks?" said the mistress. "Everyone knows he's just poor white trash from down by the crossroads."

"That may be so, Lavinia, but he's a very good manager."

"Just remember, John, *you* own this plantation.

And I wouldn't mind a bit if you got rid of that Clara."

Jordan felt sick at hearing this. Not Clara! Uriah's mom?

"Now, Lavinia," said the master, "that's been over for years. It was nothing. Besides, Clara is one of our best workers."

"Please, John." The mistress's voice went soft. "It would please me. Do it for me," she pleaded.

Jordan couldn't believe what he was hearing. Would they actually sell Uriah's mom away from her family?

The master sighed. "I'll think about it."

"Just do it," the mistress whispered, more sharply this time.

There was a pause, then he sighed. "All right, Lavinia. If it will please you."

Jordan wondered if there could be another Clara on the place.

"Thaddeus has been sickly lately," said the master. "Our climate doesn't seem to agree with him."

"He looks good when he doesn't have the fever. And he's strong and willing. He'd bring in several hundred dollars."

Listening to these people talk about a man's

selling price in dollars made Jordan feel physically ill. He closed his eyes and tried to imagine himself back in his own time. Maybe if he willed it hard enough he could get there without the watch. He pictured his home, Tachelle and Mom in the kitchen having a big bowl of cereal for breakfast, but it didn't work. He remained under the master's bed, listening, quiet as a mouse as the talk between Lavinia and John continued.

"John, what about the boy who came here with Uriah? You know, the one who followed him here from the woods?"

They were talking about *him!* Jordan! A shock pulsed through him. Don't pass out, Jordan, he told himself. Listen up, and listen hard!

"I must look into that, Lavinia. No doubt he's a runaway. I'll make some inquiries."

"Suppose no one claims him?"

"Then we can either keep him or sell him."

"If no one claims him by the time the trader comes to town, I'd say we have a perfect right to sell him. How old is he, John?"

"Oh, about twelve or thirteen."

"At that age he could bring us three hundred dollars."

Three hundred dollars! The price of a horse! Jordan's brain whirled. Every muscle and nerve in his body tightened. Cold sweat dampened his hands. It was as if he had been thrown into a shrinking iron box that was slowly crushing him to death. He wondered how the master and his wife would like it if they had to stand under a TODAY'S SPECIAL sign at Wal-Mart with price tags around their necks.

NINE

After deciding to sell
Jordan, Clara, and Thaddeus, the master and his wife finished dressing and left the room. Jordan waited until he was sure they had reached the stairway, then crawled out from under the bed. It was too risky to go out the way he came in, so he climbed out a window that opened onto a second-story balcony. Grabbing an overhanging tree branch, he shimmied down to where he could grip the thick vine running down the side of the house. He slid to the ground, then took off as fast as he could, back to the cabin. He had to tell Uriah's mom and ask her if there was another Clara on the place. And talk to Thaddeus too. Then, watch or no watch, it

was off to the woods for him. He wasn't about to stick around here and be sold. No way.

Back at the cabin Clara was still on her blanket, lying on her stomach. But Uriah was gone.

"Where's Uriah?" Jordan asked her.

"He be gone to the necessary house. He be back." Jordan figured she meant the outhouse.

"I just found out about something I think you ought to know," he said. "The master and his wife plan to sell some slaves."

"And how did you hear that?"

"I was hiding under their bed."

Clara lifted her head a little and turned toward Jordan. A slow smile spread across her face. "Hidin' under they bed?"

"Yeah. I went in there to get a hold of the master's watch, because I need it to go back to my own time. I could hear them coming, so I hid under their bed. They said they're going to sell some slaves to raise money. Are you the only Clara on this place?"

She sat up slowly, and narrowed her eyes. "Yes. I be the only Clara. Who they gonna sell?"

"You, me, and Thaddeus. They decided. I heard it all."

"You tellin' me the truth, boy?"

He crossed his heart. "So help me God."

"You willin' to swear on a Bible?"

"I am." She reached down under her blanket and pulled out the rattiest-looking Bible Jordan had ever seen. The leather cover was dirty and peeled, the spine was gone, and the brown pages stuck out every which way. To keep it from falling apart, the whole thing was tied up with frayed twine.

"Don't you say nothin' about this," she said. "The masta don't know we has it. Books is against the rules, especially the Bible. Ol' Joe say it's 'cause the Bible teach about freedom, and the masta, he be afraid we learn about it and run away. But this book, it come to me from my mama. She couldn't read, but her uncle, he read it to her when she was little, so she give it to me to remember her by. Promise me now, you won't say nothin' about it." Her uptilted eyes, so much like his mom's, pleaded with him.

"I promise."

She held that raggedy book as if it were a little baby. Watching her made Jordan want to cry. He could see how much it meant to her.

She raised the Bible up to him. "Put your hands on this book, boy." He did.

"Do you swear to God what you said was the

truth? That the masta gonna sell me and Thaddeus and you?"

"I swear it." She stared at the book for a minute, then kissed it and put it back under the blanket.

"What are you going to do?" Jordan asked.

"I don't know. I has to talk to Seth. When it come to decidin' things, he got a mighty good head on him."

"Where can I find Thaddeus?"

"If he sick, he be in the cabin. If he well, he be in the field." There was no time to waste. Jordan ran outside and tried to remember which cabin the overseer had gone into when he checked on Thaddeus. He'd try the third one on his right.

He was about to go in when he heard a woman's voice inside. He could swear it sounded like the mistress's. But what would she be doing in the quarters? He ducked into a narrow space between the cabins. He could hear her talking but couldn't understand her words. After a few minutes he peered around the corner of the cabin and saw her come out the door. She carried a black leather bag, the kind doctors in western movies used when they made house calls. She turned and walked up the road leading to the big house.

When she was out of sight, Jordan went in.

Lying on a blanket with a wet rag on his forehead was a big, strong-looking black man.

"Are you Thaddeus?"

"That be my name." Then he asked Jordan in a rumbling voice, "Who you be?"

"My name's Jordan Scott."

"Don't know that name."

"I'm new here, but I don't belong."

"Where you belong, then?"

"Never mind." Jordan didn't bother to explain.

Thaddeus smiled. "You on the run?"

"Yes," Jordan said. "And you'd better be too."

"Who says?"

"I do. I heard the master and mistress talking in the big house. They're going to sell you and Clara and me."

Thaddeus grinned. "Mistress Henning, she wouldn't sell me. She a angel of mercy. Why, she come down here every time I gets the fever and give me medicine. She was seein' to me jus' a minute ago. She a mighty kind woman."

Jordan could tell he wasn't getting through to him, and time was slipping by. "If you don't believe me, ask Clara."

"Who told her?"

"I did."

"That's what I thought." Then he let out a kind of grunt, letting Jordan know that the conversation was over.

"Talk to Clara," Jordan said. If she wanted to tell him about swearing on her Bible, that was her business. "I've got to go now."

Jordan ran as fast as he could toward the swamp woods. If he could find his way back to that tree where he'd hung his cap, he'd be fairly close to the underpass. Maybe he could break the spell without the watch and find his way home. But if he couldn't, he'd sneak back to the big house tomorrow morning before the master dressed.

Jordan hesitated at the edge of the woods, afraid to go in. Trees grew every which way, tangled with vines. The ground was choked with weeds and bushes, and was probably crawling with snakes. But if he was sold to the slave trader, he could be sent miles from here. He might lose any chance of finding his way home.

Jordan entered the woods, his heart racing, trying to remember in which direction he and Uriah had walked just two days before. The going was rough. He stumbled and fell a few times, and was unable to find the tree where he'd hung his cap. Suddenly he stopped and listened. He heard voices. The boy's voice was Uriah's, he was sure of it. Jordan crept closer and peered out from behind a bush. Uriah was talking with some old man with black wrinkled skin and long gray hair. The old man wore no clothes except a rabbit skin hanging from a rope around his waist and a baseball cap on his head. Jordan's own cap! The two of them sat on a log in a little clearing, looking at a big book.

"What's that word, Uriah?" asked the man, in a deep, hushed voice.

"God."

"Right. Now don't you forget that word, Uriah. It's God gonna lead us to freedom. He led the Israelites outta Egypt. They was slaves—just like us. Someday he gonna lead us out too." He closed the book. "You better be gettin' on back, 'fore the paddyrollers catch you."

"You gonna teach me again next week, Ol' Joe?"

"As long as I be alive, I gonna teach, so I be waitin'."

That's why Uriah had the chills and fever once a week! So he could run off to the woods for reading lessons. That boy was risking his life to learn. Jordan was amazed at his courage and sorry he wouldn't be able to tell him good-bye. Uriah's whole family had been good to him. He would miss them.

Uriah dashed off, and Old Joe slowly got up off the log. Poor guy was nearly bent double; you could tell it was hard for him to walk. Jordan decided that he had to talk the old man into leading him back to that tree where he'd found the cap. He shadowed Old Joe through the woods until he hobbled over to what looked like a dead bush and pushed it to one side. He was about to disappear into what looked like a cave.

"Old Joe?" Jordan said.

"Who there?"

Jordan came out to where the old man could see him. "I need help."

"You a runaway?" he asked.

"Well, yes and no."

"Come in." He beckoned Jordan inside the cave, and pulled the dead bush in front of the opening. It was nearly pitch-dark in there, but Jordan wasn't afraid. He could tell Old Joe was a good man.

"Now, boy," he said. "Tell me your story."

Jordan did the best he could. He told him everything, from the time he took Grandpa's watch right up to the present minute. The old man listened, and didn't make fun of Jordan the way the others had. Sometimes he'd say "Hmmm." Then Jordan told him about hanging his cap on the tree.

"Ah, this here cap!" Old Joe took it off his head and stared at it. "I reckon it done brought us together." He handed it to Jordan.

Jordan wasn't sure what he meant by that, but at least he wasn't laughing at his story. "So, what do you think?" he asked the old man.

"I think you be brought here for a reason," he said.

"What reason?"

"In time, you will learn."

"But I gotta get out of here right now. They're going to sell me. I need you to lead me back to that tree where you found my cap. Can you do that? Please?"

"Come, then." The old man struggled to his knees, and he and Jordan crawled out of the cave. Old Joe shoved the bush back over the hole and grabbed a crooked tree branch for a cane. They walked for what must have been half an hour, stopping every now and then so that the old man could rest. Suddenly, in the distance, Jordan recognized the tree with the stretched-out black branches that looked like arms. When they got close, he saw the muddy place where he and Uriah had searched for the watch.

"What you gonna do now?" asked Old Joe.

"I don't know. What would you do?"

"You could hang the cap back on the tree, then see if it help you go back to your own time."

Jordan did that, then stared at the cap and waited. Nothing happened. Without the watch, he wasn't really surprised.

"When I got here," Jordan said, "I walked to the tree from that direction." He pointed.

"Why don't you go back that way?" Old Joe suggested. "I be waitin' here, watchin'."

It was comforting to have Old Joe along. Jordan paced out what he thought the distance was to the underpass. There was nothing but woods as far as he could see. He looked back, and there stood Old Joe in the distance, half hidden in the underbrush. Then he heard the clopping of horses' hooves in the distance. The paddyrollers!

"Joe!" Jordan yelled. "Joe!" He ran to the place where he'd last seen Old Joe, but he had vanished. He'd probably heard the horses too, and hid somewhere. Jordan should've kept his mouth shut. If he'd stayed cool he might have had a chance, but there he stood, right out in plain sight. The paddyrollers rode over to where he stood. There were two this time, the same two he and Uriah had seen, but the blond one was missing.

"Hey, boy!" one said. "Lemme see your pass."

"I lost it," Jordan said.

"What's your name, boy?" asked the other one.

"Jordan Henning." He left off the Scott this time. If they thought he belonged to the Hennings, they might let him off more easily.

"What you doin' out here in the swamp woods at cotton-pickin' time?" one asked him. He didn't give Jordan time to answer and said, "I gotta take you back to your master, boy." He tied a rope around Jordan's waist and fastened the other end to his saddle. Then he rode at a trot, with Jordan alongside him, running like crazy. The other guy followed, his horse's hot breath on Jordan's neck.

TEN

At the big house the master paid off the paddyrollers. Then he tied Jordan's rope to his saddle and, with Jordan at his side, rode out to the field where he gave the overseer orders to whip him. The master did it in such a gentle, soft-spoken way that Jordan thought he could have been ordering a meal at a fancy restaurant.

Buster was standing nearby. After the master left, Buster said to the overseer, "Sir, what good it gonna do to whip a hand when he could be pickin'? Why not whip him tonight after he done finished workin'?" Jordan hoped and prayed that Buster would do the whipping and that he'd do it the way he had the night before. But, knowing it was unlikely he'd be that lucky twice, his empty stomach rolled and swirled.

"You're right, Buster. Put him to work and whip him later. It's Saturday. He'll be back on his feet by Monday." So they put him on a row of cotton and gave him a sack.

Jordan was careful this time not to pull off the bolls or break the branches. At noon Seth gave Jordan half of his corn cake. He was still starving, but was grateful for the man's kindness. They worked on and on through the blazing afternoon until after sunset. Whenever he felt like blacking out, Jordan put his head down until he felt better. No way was he going to risk another field whipping.

After weighing time Travis told Buster to take Jordan out and give him ten lashes for running away and picking slow. While they walked to the whipping post, Buster chewed Jordan out. Jordan was positive that the driver was really going to beat him this time. Then, while he tied Jordan's hands, Buster whispered in his ear.

"This be the last time I gonna let you off easy, boy. Next time you misbehaves, you gonna pay and pay hard." Jordan prayed several "Thank you, Gods" and screamed while Buster cracked the whip on the ground.

When he limped back toward the cabin in the dark, Jordan knew he should hide in the woods, but couldn't bring himself to go into that wild place alone at night. He wondered if Clara and Thaddeus had already left. Outside the quarters the slaves were all dressed up in bright colors, the young girls wearing ribbons in their hair. Everybody was singing and shouting.

"What's going on?" Jordan asked Seth.

Seth grinned. "It's Saturday night, boy. And they's a dance at the shack on the river bottom.

What was Seth doing anyway, looking so happy, as if he didn't have a care in the world? Didn't he know that Clara was going to be sold? Jordan wondered if she hadn't told him yet. "A dance? You're going to a dance?"

"We gonna kick up our heels," he said, "and you better come too, boy."

Jordan thought it was about time these people had a little fun and he was glad for them, but he wasn't about to stick around and be sold. No way. Besides, he had to pretend he was hurt from the whipping.

"I can't go," Jordan said.

"What you mean you can't go?"

"I've been whipped."

"Was it Buster whipped you?"

Jordan nodded.

Uriah's dad smiled again. "We all understands. You just pick up your feet and come along."

"What if Buster's there and sees me?"

"The driver, he don't mix with the field hands."

"What if Travis sees me?"

"He won't be there. Just come along when you ready." Seth seemed too happy. Jordan didn't want to be the one to break the news to him about Clara. If she was still here, he'd have to ask her what was going on. When he went into the cabin, Clara was tying a blue scarf around her neck.

"You told Seth yet? About being sold?" Jordan asked.

A cloud passed over her face. "Yes. I tol' him."

"Then why are you still hanging around here?"

"He don't believe you."

"Did you tell him I swore on the Bible?"

"Yes. But he still think you moonstruck."

"I know what I heard. You believe me, don't you?"

"Maybe you misunderstands. Whyn't you go tell Seth exac'ly what you tol' me." So Jordan went back outside and took Seth behind the cabin and explained to him just what he'd told Clara.

"She done tol' me all about that," he said. "She say you hid under the masta's bed." Then he laughed and shook his head. "Boy, you act mighty crazy. You is moonstruck, boy. Moonstruck." Jordan could tell that Seth just couldn't believe his story.

So here they were, hanging around the plantation when they should have been long gone. But maybe he could use the party to make his getaway.

Jordan went back inside the cabin and found Uriah putting on a pair of bright red pants.

"Where'd you get those fancy pants?" Jordan asked.

"From the big house. The mistress, she send old clothes to the quarters sometimes."

Jordan felt sorry that he didn't have anything dressed-up to wear. He went out to the well, drew up a bucket of water, and tried to wash off the field dirt. It was the best he could do. His plan was all worked out. He'd go to the dance, and while everybody was busy having a good time, he'd hide out nearby. Then he'd sneak into the big house early in the morning and grab the watch. If the watch didn't send him back home immediately, then he'd run to the woods and get Old Joe to lead him to the tree where he'd hung his cap. If he could just put those two things together, he'd soon be home. For the first time since he had hid out under that bed, Jordan felt relaxed and even hopeful. In the meantime he decided to enjoy himself.

It was quite a parade. Slaves, all sizes and ages, sang and hollered on the way to the dance. As they walked along, a man by the name of Silas played the banjo.

"What about the paddyrollers?" Jordan asked Uriah. "Won't they hear us and come and get us?"

"We fixed the paddyrollers one night last spring, and they ain't bothered our dances since then."

"What happened?"

"We tied ropes to the trees and stretched 'em across the road. And when they came gallopin' in the dark to get us they was thrown clean off their horses. You never heard such yellin' and cussin' in your life. They ain't been back. Everybody know we has these dances on Saturday night. The masta, he pretend he don't know. And slaves from the other plantations comes too."

Jordan never saw a group of people so happy. When he asked why, Uriah explained that tomorrow, bein' Sunday, they wouldn't be waked up by the overseer's horn. They'd have a little time off.

Jordan was glad for them, but he was determined not to be around to see it.

Uriah and Jordan laughed and teased and roughhoused as they walked through weeds and brambles. Uriah was quick and bright and full of fun. He seemed more and more like a little brother and Jordan knew that if and when he was able to go back to his own time he was really going to miss him.

"Hey," Jordan said to him, "suppose I find that hole in my time box and pass through? How about you coming with me?"

Uriah giggled. "Where they have all that 'lectricity?"

"Yeah."

Uriah didn't answer, because in the distance they heard the thump thump of music, and everybody had stopped talking to listen. Pretty soon they came to a run-down old shack. The broken windows glowed out at them in the moonlight. The tall yard weeds grew up through the wooden porch steps. They creaked and groaned as the slaves climbed them.

Inside, lanterns shone and it was somehow the cheeriest place Jordan had ever seen. Somebody played a fiddle and another played the banjo. Two men, sitting with their backs together, straddled a drum made out of a barrel with animal skins stretched across each end. And could they beat that drum! Another guy ran a stick across the teeth of some animal's jawbone. It was the craziest, wildest music Jordan had ever heard. Uriah and Jordan looked at each other and grinned. Their feet just flew up off the floor and they both started dancing around in circles. People laughed and sang and whooped and hollered. And Jordan couldn't believe the food. Several women were busy putting it out on a long table. There was so much! Somebody had brought a ham and several people had brought fried chicken.

Jordan asked one of the women where it had all come from.

She threw back her head and laughed. "The masta's smokehouse ain't always locked."

"And the overseer, he can't be guardin' the henhouse at cotton-pickin' time," said another, "and the Lord, He done look the other way, 'cause He know we work for that food fair and square." There was corn bread, a sweet potato pie, fried okra, turnip greens, and black-eyed peas. Jordan couldn't wait to devour it all.

After supper a dance contest called "settin' the floor" started. A man took a burnt corncob and drew a circle on the dance floor about three feet across. First one couple and then another tried to dance without touching the line. Jordan decided that it must have been harder than it looked, because one couple after another stepped on that line and had to quit. Somebody had a clock and kept time. The ones that danced the longest were going to win the cake that sat on the table like a tall white tower. One look at that cake and Jordan made up his mind that he was going to win.

All of a sudden the music stopped. The master walked through the room with three white men. A hush fell over the crowd as two of the men seized Clara, the other grabbed Jordan, and both were dragged out the door. Jordan was so surprised that all he thought of in that moment was that he'd probably never get to taste that cake. Clara screamed and called out, "Seth!" Seth and the rest of her family, including Uriah in his bright red pants, followed her out, the children yelling, "Mama! Mama!" Jordan's next thoughts were about the watch and Uriah and Mom and Tachelle and Grandpa. His dad too.

ELEVEN

When they dragged Jordan
and Clara to the wagon, Thaddeus was already there, lying down with his hands behind his back and his ankles roped together.

"Where are we going?" Jordan asked one of the men who was tying his hands and feet—but he got no answer. He felt wobbly and light-headed, knowing that his chances of getting back home grew slimmer by the minute. He watched as one man held Clara down while another tied her up.

"Seth! Seth!" she cried. "Uriah! Rabe! My baby Ella! You can't take me away from my family. You can't! It ain't right!" Jordan was terrified for himself, not knowing what would happen next, but he felt even worse for Clara and her family. Poor Uriah was sobbing and yelling. Who wouldn't? He was losing his mom! And she was such a good person too, someone who helped everybody around her. While they tied them up, Seth and all of his kids screamed and tried to climb into the wagon with Clara. Then one of the three men pointed his shotgun at them and herded them away. Thaddeus lay there, crying and moaning.

"I shoulda listened to you, boy," he said to Jordan. "You was right. They gonna sell us, sure enough."

With the three of them tied up, the wagon's driver took off on a bumpy path. A few stragglers from the party watched but most ran off. Sitting in back, watching over them, was a white man holding a shotgun. If only they'd tied Jordan's hands in front, he might have chewed himself free, but no such luck. Besides, the guy with the gun didn't take his eyes off them for a second. The bright moonlight didn't help either. But Jordan made up his mind to run away the first chance he got. No matter what.

After a long jerky ride they pulled up to a big barnlike building. The white man untied Jordan's ankles and led him inside. A lantern threw a shadowy light over a big room. Jordan couldn't believe what he saw. On one side of the room there must have been twenty or thirty black guys all chained together. Some sat; others were lying down. Many moaned and cried. On the other side there were about the same number of women and girls, held together with ropes. They were crying too. Between the two groups a dozing white man sat with a pistol on his lap. He woke up when they came in.

"Three for the coffle," said the guy who held Jordan. "One boy here, one man and one woman in the wagon." Was "coffle" another word for coffin? Hey, Jordan told himself, these traders couldn't sell dead bodies. Keep your head. You have to think your way out of this.

The guy with the pistol handed the other one something that looked like a huge iron doughnut with a padlock on it. The other guy undid the padlock and clamped the heavy thing around Jordan's neck.

"Look!" Jordan said. "You can't do this! I'm *not* a slave!" Then he went into his explanation about how he belonged in another century. While he talked, the man led him over to where the other men were chained together and fastened his neck doughnut to the chain on another man's collar. The guards chained Jordan's right wrist to the other guy's left wrist. They were shackled together, two by two. Then all the pairs were linked to one another by a long chain that ran through each man's neck padlock. Escape would be impossible.

When the guard hammered the wrist bolt into an iron staple, Jordan yelled, "Hey, man, that hurts." The guard then poked him in the stomach with the butt of his shotgun.

"If you think this hurts, boy," the man said, "you just keep up that silly talk of yours and we'll show you what real hurt is all about." Fear and rage shot through Jordan.

When they brought Thaddeus in and chained him, he didn't say a word. But when they tied Clara down, she screamed.

"Seth!" she cried. "Seth! Come get me! Come!" Then she sobbed. When Jordan heard her, tears ran down his face. He sat there in those terrible chains for what seemed like hours. When the man he was chained to decided to lie down, his chains pulled Jordan down too. Since it hurt to move, he lay very still and may have even slept a little.

In the morning when they sat up to eat the cornmeal mush they'd been given, Jordan noticed that Thaddeus wasn't eating. His eyes looked strange, kind of blank. When Jordan spoke to him he didn't seem to hear. Jordan thought that he must have that fever again.

"Hey, mister," Jordan said to the man with the pistol, "Thaddeus over there is sick. He needs some medicine."

The man sneered at him. "He ain't the first puny one we had, and he probably ain't gonna be the last." The way he spoke reminded Jordan of King somehow. But this guy was white. It didn't make sense. Nothing made sense now.

"Can't you give him some medicine?" Jordan asked.

He turned on Jordan, twirling his pistol. "When I want your advice, boy, I'll ask for it. We got ways of dealin' with niggers what speak outta turn." Jordan was so angry that he wanted to fly out of those chains and strangle him. But he just clenched his teeth and watched while poor Thaddeus lay there helpless, his eyes glazed over.

Clara wasn't doing much better. She was still

crying, calling out to Seth and the kids until the guard swatted her across the back with a paddle that had holes the size of quarters drilled through it. Jordan closed his eyes. How could they do that? How could they! When he looked again, Clara had stopped yelling, but she was heaving huge quiet sobs. The man hung the strange paddle on the stained and peeling wall.

"Funny-looking paddle," Jordan whispered to the man he was chained to.

"They uses a paddle with holes so it don't leave no scars. Nobody gonna buy a nigger with whip scars. They figures if a nigger been whipped, he done made trouble." This guy seemed to know what he was talking about.

"What's a coffle?" Jordan asked him.

The man smiled. "It's what you see right here, boy. You is in a coffle. 'Nother name for chain gang."

Jordan had seen pictures of prison chain gangs. "How long are they going to keep us chained?"

"Till we gets to market, I reckon."

"When will that be?" Icy fingers of fear crawled up Jordan's neck.

"Boy, you know as much as I do."

"How long you been chained?"

"Three days and three nights. Days we walks. Nights we gets to lay down. My name's Caleb. What's yours?"

"Jordan. Where'd you come from?"

"Louisiana. Whatever you do, boy, don't let 'em sell you down the river. Things is bad in them rice swamps. You bend over all day with your feet in the water, snakes swimmin' all around. If you don't gets moccasin bit, you gets the water sores. Mississippi and Louisiana, they's off my list for good. Give me cotton or tobacco any day." It was hard for Jordan to imagine anything worse than the cotton fields. But when he looked down at the man's swollen ankles and the sores oozing all over his feet, Jordan knew that there was.

By the time they finished their cornmeal mush it was getting light. Four armed guards, two white and two black, stood them up and led them out the door and down a dirt road. It was drizzling. In a few minutes Jordan was wet and chilled to the bone. He shivered and his teeth chattered.

"You can be glad it ain't hot," Caleb said. "The heat's a heap worse'n the cold." Jordan looked back and saw Thaddeus stumble along, barely able to walk. He couldn't see Clara because all the women marched behind the men. The chains clanked and rattled. The iron collar was heavy against Jordan's shoulders and rubbed his neck raw. The chains cut his wrist. He tried not to move his head and to keep step with Caleb, who had longer legs than he did. Jordan couldn't imagine how that man had been able to march three days and three nights with his ankles and feet so swollen and raw.

Even at noontime they still didn't stop. They just kept following the back of the wagon where the two white armed guards watched over them. There were two black guards who marched behind them and sometimes alongside them. Jordan wondered why blacks were doing that job, but he figured that they must be slaves too, just obeying orders. He was so tired and hungry and aching that he didn't know how he could walk another step, but as he put one foot in front of the other, he counted his steps into the thousands. Somehow it helped.

That afternoon Jordan felt the chains pull him backward and there was a scuffling sound behind him. The wagon stopped, and so did the marchers.

The two white men jumped off the wagon and ran behind them. Jordan turned to look. It was Thaddeus. His head was thrown back, eyes wide open, feet dragging on the ground. He was held up by his iron collar and neck chains. One of the white guards checked his breathing and the other one felt his wrist.

"He's dead," one said. "We'll have to bury him. Tell Jeb and Rollo to start diggin'."

The two black guards grabbed shovels from the wagon and dug a shallow grave. When they took off Thaddeus's chains, laid him in the ground, and shoveled dirt over him, tears rolled down Jordan's cheeks, but he was careful not to make a sound. Nobody read a Bible verse or said a prayer. They just buried him like an animal. Silently they all watched, too scared to say anything.

When the guards put their shovels back in the wagon, one of the marchers sang out in a rich, deep voice, "The Lord bless and keep him." Other voices said, "Amen." Then somebody started humming. The guards didn't pay any attention, and soon others joined in. They walked along singing one hymn or spiritual after another. Jordan listened to the voices rise and blend in harmony. The sound was oddly beautiful and he was able to forget his fear and pain for minutes at a time. It was as if they all knew that they couldn't let Thaddeus give up his life without some kind of a goodbye. Jordan didn't know who that brave soul was who spoke those first words, but he knew he'd never forget that moment.

TWELVE

By sunset Jordan's neck
and wrist were raw and bleeding, and his shoulders and feet were in such pain that he thought it might be a relief to do what Thaddeus had done and just die on the spot. A couple of hours later they marched into a town and stopped in front of a huge wooden building with barred windows. It looked like a jail. From the outside the building appeared to take up the whole block, but when Jordan and the others went through the gate, they came into a kind of courtyard with the building surrounding it on all four sides; the windows looking out on the courtyard were barred too. Jordan was glad they were stopping, but when he saw

those windows, he knew that it wasn't a good place. Several men, black and white both, met the slaves in the yard. Two had guns. They undid the chains on the men in front of Jordan, then took them through a door into the building. What that door led to, Jordan could hardly stand to think about. Some of the men were so weak that they swayed and stumbled, barely able to walk. The gravel on the grounds cut into Jordan's sore feet.

When his turn came, Jordan was taken into a big room where the men ahead of him sat eating at a long table loaded with food. There was bread, bacon, potatoes, and beans. Jordan was starving and sat down to eat right away.

Soon Caleb came in and sat down beside him. "You know why they feedin' us like this, dontcha?" he said to Jordan.

Jordan didn't care. "No. Why?"

"The traders, they wants us to look fed and sassy when they puts us up on the block in a few days."

"How do you know?" Jordan asked him.

"Been through it before."

"What else are they gonna do to us?"

"I dunno. Every slave pen is different, but ain't none of 'em good."

Jordan and the others in his chain gang spent three nights and two days in the slave pen. Nights, they slept on the floor. No mattress, no blanket, no sheets, nothing between them and the hard packed dirt. But Jordan was so glad to be out of those chains that it didn't seem half bad. Days, the guards and their helpers buzzed around them trying to make them look good for the buyers. They took Jordan's burlap clothes away and gave him a pair of pants and a shirt. The sorry-looking secondhand clothes didn't really fit, but the fact that they weren't as scratchy on his raw skin was a big relief.

Jordan kept trying to tell everybody he met that he didn't belong here, but by now he wasn't surprised that nobody believed him. Uriah and Old Joe were the only ones in this slave world who ever had, and God only knew if he would ever see them again.

Almost all the slaves in the pen were barefoot, but if a slave came in with shoes on he was allowed to keep them. Jordan couldn't stop thinking about his Nikes. But because of the way the driver had treated him, he didn't feel too bad about Buster getting them. If it hadn't been for Buster, he'd probably be dead from the whip.

The way the men in charge fussed over them, it seemed to Jordan that they were getting the slaves ready for a beauty contest. They were all given a scrubbing, had their hair and nails trimmed, and were taught how to walk, stand up straight, and smile. After Jordan went through the slave pen door that first night, he never saw Clara. They separated the men and women right away. He hoped that she felt better, but how could she when she had been torn away from her whole family?

Jordan watched a black guy try to pluck the gray hairs out of a slave's head. He wondered again why a black man was doing the plucking, but he supposed he must be a slave just like the others, working for the trader. Another one was putting black dye on an old man's graying hair. Then Jordan and the others had lines to memorize, as if they were practicing for a play.

"What can you do?" A white man was giving Jordan his cue. "Now stand up straight and look me in the eye when you answer."

"I can pick cotton," Jordan said. He didn't have to say how slow he was.

"What else?"

Jordan couldn't think of anything else. In this world he felt as helpless as a baby. The man sneered in disgust. Jordan thought of something. "I can read and write," he offered.

The man frowned. "You better keep quiet about that, boy. It ain't legal for niggers to read and write in this state."

The white man went on to quiz the next slave in line, and said to Jordan over his shoulder, "You better think of somethin' else you can do, like hoein' and plantin' and drivin' a team. I'll be comin' 'round again, and you better have some right smart answers ready, boy." Jordan decided that if he was going to live through this, he'd have to come up with some "right smart" lies.

After several days of eating, sleeping, practicing their lines, and having their skin washed and oiled, the slaves were ready for the big sale. Everybody looked and acted nervous. Jordan didn't know how he could go through with it, but he couldn't see any way out. Guards and guns were everywhere. The morning of the auction the head trader was hopping around rubbing his hands. He inspected all the slaves several times, making sure they looked good and knew what to say.

Jordan and the others watched from the barred windows while the white buyers swarmed into the gravel courtyard. In the middle of it was a platform about three feet square and two feet high with steps on the side. Then the barred doors were opened and Jordan marched out with the others, single file. Altogether there were about thirty of them. As they stood lined up along the building, facing the platform, Jordan glanced at the white people. He couldn't believe that any one of these strangers could have such power over his life. What if he ended up in a place even worse than the Henning plantation? Hopelessness dragged at him. He knew he'd never see Mom and his dad and Tachelle and Grandpa again. Never! If only he could have just one more chance to say good-bye.

One of the doors on the other side of the yard opened and the women marched out of their building and stood in a line facing the men. There was Clara. She glanced at Jordan but didn't smile or offer any kind of greeting. Her jaw was set, and in her eyes was a steely glint.

The white people got up from their benches and walked up and down the two rows. Some asked the slaves to open their mouths so that they could inspect their teeth. A short man with a reddish-colored beard came up to Jordan and asked his name and what he could do.

"Jordan Henning Scott," he said, "and I can pick cotton, take care of horses, drive a team, and do whatever you want, sir." He hoped that before he had to prove any of that, he'd get his chance to run away. If someone bought him, he could escape more easily than he could here in the market. But Jordan guessed the man wasn't interested, because he walked over to the other side and started talking to Clara.

A little later one of the white guards announced in a loud voice, "The auction is about to begin. Everybody gather 'round." The people bunched up around the platform while a guard brought the first black man up the steps and told him, under his breath, to "Stand up smart, now."

The head trader started talking fast in a loud voice. "We have a fine young man here, folks. His former owner said he was honest and a hard worker. He has done fieldwork, blacksmithing, brick making, and a little carpentry. You can see for yourselves, folks, he's a fine specimen of a man." Then he turned to the slave and said, "Take off your shirt, boy, and show 'em your muscles."

The slave did as he was told. His brown muscles were shiny with oil and rippled in the sun. "Yes, folks, this black buck was made for hard work." The trader turned to him again. "Show 'em your back, boy." He obeyed. "Now, folks, this young man has no whip scars. That shows he's well behaved. He's a good, obedient servant, one that'll be loyal and give you good service for many years to come. Do I hear a bid? The man with the blue coat over there, what do you bid?"

"Nine hundred, sir."

"Only nine hundred? Fine specimen like this? Do I hear eleven?"

"Eleven twenty-five," said another man.

"I hear eleven twenty-five. Good man like this oughta bring fifteen hundred, easy."

"Twelve hundred," another said.

"We have a bid for twelve hundred," said the auctioneer, "do I hear a bid for twelve fifty?" Silence. "No? Come on now, folks, we can't let a prime hand like this go for a mere twelve hundred." The guy waited, but the bids stopped. "Gone to the highest bidder. Twelve hundred dollars." A white man dressed in a fancy gray suit paid his money to the auctioneer, and the black man on the platform stepped down and went off through the courtyard door with his new owner.

The horror of what he'd just seen hit Jordan like a speeding train and made him sick with fear and outrage. He remembered hearing about the slave auctions from Grandpa and in his history books, but it had never seemed real. He wanted to scream out for them to stop, but he knew he'd just be hauled off to the whipping room. They'd showed the slaves the whipping room when they first arrived, and the iron rings in the floor for tying them down. Jordan took deep breaths to try and calm himself.

The auction went on for hours. The slaves stepped up to the platform, one by one. Out of about twelve or thirteen so far, all were sold except for two nobody wanted. Somebody took them back into the building. Jordan couldn't help wondering what would happen to them. And he hoped he wouldn't have to find out. It was hot in the yard with no trees to shade them, and the guards finally told them they could sit down on the ground to wait their turn.

When Clara stepped up on the platform, she looked different. Her eyes flashed, her jaw jutted out, and her chest heaved. She looked angry enough to kill, and Jordan could understand why. The auctioneer went into a long speech about what she had done, some of it lies.

"Take a good look at this woman here," the auctioneer said, "she's a good breeder. She's had ten children and is good for that many more." Back at the Henning place Jordan had counted only six. But maybe she'd had four others before Henning bought her. Maybe she'd been torn away from a whole other family. It's not like there was anything to keep it from happening, over and over. The possibility of it haunted him. This woman who looked so much like his own mom! How different their lives had been. His mom had gone to school nights, landed a good job, and bought a terrific house in a nice neighborhood. Both she and Clara probably had about the same brainpower. But for Clara there was no future at all.

"She's a fine cook," the auctioneer went on, "and an excellent housekeeper." The only thing Jordan had ever seen her cook was corn cake and salt pork, but maybe she had been a cook at one time, or a housekeeper, and then got sent out to the cotton fields.

"She's strong and well built. She'd do equally well as a fieldworker or a house servant."

One of the men in the crowd yelled up at Clara, "Bare yourself to the waist, girl, so we can see how well you're built."

Clara put her hands on her hips and her up-tilted eyes sparked with anger. "I picks cotton fast as any man, cooks up a good supper, and I does any chores that needs doin'—and that's all you needs to know."

Jordan was astonished at how she stood up for herself. But he also knew that she was probably so heartbroken that a part of her didn't care anymore what happened to her. He was surprised when, instead of hauling her off to the whipping room, the auctioneer laughed.

"Haw, haw, haw! It seems that Miss Modesty here has an uncommon spirit. But, folks, it's often the feisty ones that turn out to be the best work-ers. What am I bid?"

"Five hundred," said the red-bearded man who had earlier talked to Jordan and Clara in the lineup.

"Five hundred for this fine servant is an insult," said the auctioneer. "Do I hear seven hundred?" Silence. Then somebody spoke up from the back.

"Seven hundred, sir."

The red-bearded man spoke up again. "Seven twenty-five."

"Seven fifty," said another.

"Eight hundred," someone else shouted. After that nobody said a word, but the auctioneer kept trying to drive up the price. Jordan was doing his best to stay cool, but the ache in his throat was killing him. He kept seeing his own mom up there on the auction block in Clara's place, and tears slid down his face. Finally the auctioneer gave up and Clara walked off with her new owner for eight hundred dollars. "Please, God," Jordan prayed, "let him be a kind man."

When Jordan's turn came, he was a nervous wreck. He trembled all over and blinked back tears. He stood up there on that platform, bracing himself for all the auctioneer's lies.

"Folks, step right up and take a good look at this fine young man. He's only twelve years old. A good age for training him any way you want. This young man already knows how to plant and pick cotton, drive a team, and take care of horses. He's tall and strong for his age. He's a fast learner too. What do you bid?"

"Three hundred dollars," said the red-bearded man. The crowd had thinned out by now.

"Do I hear any more bids? This young fella oughta be worth at least three hundred and fifty." Silence. The auctioneer must have sensed that there was little interest, because he let Jordan go for three hundred dollars.

Following the red-bearded man through the courtyard door and out onto the street, Jordan searched frantically for a way to make his getaway. He could tell that he was expected to follow the man to his wagon or carriage, but he suddenly turned and ran off in the opposite direction. When Jordan heard the man run after him, he ducked into a yard and hid behind a bush. But the man quickly found him.

"Jordan," he said, "I don't blame you for running, but I think you'd be better off coming with me."

"I'm not a slave!" he said.

"I know," he whispered.

"You know? Then why did you buy me?"

"Shh!" He kept on whispering. "To give you your freedom."

"My freedom? I'm already free."

"At this time, and in this place, no colored person is free without freedom papers to prove it."

"So? What's this all about?"

"I'm going to give you a chance to earn your freedom papers, and then a way to escape if you're willing to make the trip."

Jordan stared at him openmouthed.

The man continued, "You see, my name is McAllen and I'm a worker with the Underground Railroad. Ever heard of it?"

"Some," said Jordan.

"It's a whole group of people, blacks and whites, who try to free the slaves. If the folks around here ever found out what I was doing, I'd likely get shot."

Jordan stared at him in disbelief. What was a white man doing freeing slaves? It didn't make sense. Then the man smiled at him and patted him on the back. "It's all right," he said. "Just come along with me, and I'll explain everything." People around here lied so much that Jordan wasn't sure he could trust the guy, but right now the man seemed to be his best bet. Jordan followed him out onto the street where his wagon was parked, climbed up, and sat on the seat next to him.

"Remember Old Joe?" the man asked.

"Sure, I remember him." How did this man know Old Joe?

"Well, Old Joe told me to buy Clara, but if I couldn't, I was to buy you. We're short of funds right now, so lucky for you, I had to buy you instead of Clara."

If this man was telling the truth, Jordan found himself feeling both lucky and sorry, saddened that he was taking the chance for freedom meant for Clara. "What do I have to do to earn my freedom papers?" he asked.

"I'll let Old Joe explain that to you."

"Where are we going?"

"First, to my farm, which is just a short way from the Henning plantation. Then we'll find Old Joe and let him tell you the rest."

So Jordan was going back to where he had a chance of getting the watch! It was a miracle!

THIRTEEN

On their long ride

McAllen told Jordan how the Underground Railroad worked. Every night he and his wife put a lit candle in their window. When runaways, often tipped off by fellow slaves, saw it, they'd come to their door and give the password "I'm a friend of a friend." The McAllens would give them food, a place to sleep, and then tell them how to go on to the next safe house with a candle in the window. On and on they'd go, usually at night to lessen the chance of being caught. If they reached certain places in the North, people would hide them and send them to Canada, where they'd be free.

"It used to be a lot easier," McAllen said.

"How?"

"Time was when the slaves would be free the minute they set foot on northern soil. But a year or so ago the country reinforced the Fugitive Slave Law. It says runaways can be captured in the North and sent back to their owners. Some people have made a nice business of catching runaways and collecting reward money. But Canada doesn't have that law, so that's where the slaves have to go now."

"That's terrible," Jordan said.

"That's the truth," McAllen said quietly. "It surely is."

Jordan studied the man's face. He could hardly believe that here was a white man willing to risk his life to help blacks. And that blacks and whites worked together to make all this happen.

"Do all the runaways make it to freedom?" Jordan asked.

"Oh, no," he whispered. "Just the lucky ones."

"What happens to the others?"

"Some are captured and sent back. Others die on the way from sickness, injury, or exposure. It's a very risky business."

"Yeah," Jordan said. He'd made up his mind about one thing. He was going to get that watch and try to go home. But if he couldn't, he would try and make it to freedom, even if it killed him. Some things were worth dying for.

It was nighttime when they reached their destination. First McAllen unhitched and fed his horses. Then he took Jordan into his house, where his wife closed the window curtains and gave them some supper. It was a small, cheerful farmhouse, and the food was good. Afterward McAllen told Jordan that he was ready to take him to Old Joe's place.

"Tonight?" Jordan was hoping that they'd let him sleep here and go to Old Joe's in the morning. He wasn't exactly crazy about walking through that swamp woods, especially at night.

"We must go now," McAllen told him. "The need is urgent."

"What do you mean?" Jordan asked.

"I think Old Joe should explain."

The waning moon dappled their path with a faint light as Jordan and McAllen entered the swamp woods. As they walked along, the underbrush rustled, animals scuttled nearby, and twigs snapped. The noises shook Jordan's nerves.

He grabbed McAllen's arm. "What was that?"

"Some small animal. It's nothing."

Off in the distance, there rang out the weirdest sound Jordan had ever heard. He must have tightened his grip on McAllen's arm.

McAllen patted his hand. "Just an old screech owl."

After what seemed like ages, Old Joe met them in front of his cave. He looked shocked when he saw Jordan with McAllen. "I be glad for you, but awful sorry 'bout Clara," he told Jordan when McAllen explained that she'd been sold. "I be prayin' for her. But none of us know why the Lord let bad things happen."

"Our job *would* be easier with Clara," McAllen replied, "but we'll have to make the best of things with the young man here." Jordan hoped and prayed that whatever he had to do it wouldn't involve walking through that forest alone at night.

When McAllen left, Jordan went inside the cave. Old Joe lit a string floating in a shallow pan of grease, then they sat among the flickering shadows.

"It's Uriah," Old Joe said. "Seth and his brothers and sisters are waitin' for him in a secret place, but he won't come, and they can't wait much longer."

"You mean they're running away?"

"Shhh! Keep your voice down. Them paddy-rollers is everywhere."

Jordan nodded.

Old Joe continued. "You has to go to Uriah and bring him here tonight. He won't want to come, but you must use everything you has to convince him that this chance at freedom is more important than anything."

"Where is he?"

"Inside the big house."

"The big house? What's he doing there?"

"It's a strange story. I don't have time to tell it now, but you'll hear it from him." Fear was zigzagging up Jordan's spine. He would have to walk through the forest, and there were the dogs in the backyard and . . .

"He sleeps on a pad outside the master's bedroom."

"What?" Jordan couldn't believe his ears. "Since when?"

"Since yesterday. I gonna lead you to the plantation grounds and wait for you at the edge of the woods." Jordan breathed a grateful sigh of relief.

"We has to go *now*," Old Joe told him, "and when you comes back with Uriah, I gonna lead the two of you to the secret place."

Fear and excitement whirled in Jordan's brain. There were so many disasters waiting to happen! But on the other hand, if he made it to the master's bedroom, the watch could be his! It was the chance he'd been waiting for. He didn't dare think about what could happen if he got caught.

With his heart thumping, Jordan and Old Joe tramped through the woods to the spooky music of frogs, crickets, screech owls, and crackling twigs. He was relieved to reach the grounds of the big house—even though he knew that the scariest part still lay ahead.

"I gonna wait for you right here," said Old Joe. "God be with you and Uriah too." His words had a comforting ring to them. "God be with you and Uriah too" echoed through Jordan's head as he climbed the hill to the big house.

Jordan crept up the front steps. The dogs made entry through the back impossible. He slowly tried to turn the knob on the front door, but it was locked. No lamplight shone downstairs. Everyone must already be in bed. There was a ground-floor window that opened like a door. It wasn't locked! Jordan climbed in. So far, so good, but he could feel his breath coming hard and his hands getting clammy. He found the stairs and tiptoed up. He was glad that he generally knew his way around, and that the floors were partly carpeted. There were no lights anywhere. The upstairs hall was pitch-dark. Jordan inched along, stopping when he heard another person's breathing. He slowly moved forward until he almost stepped on somebody sleeping by the master's door. It had to be Uriah. Jordan quickly reached down and clapped his hand over the boy's mouth.

When Uriah woke up, Jordan breathed into his ear. "Don't make a sound. It's me—Jordan."

"Jordan! What you doin' here?" he whispered. "I thought you done been sold."

"Shhh! I'll tell you later. But first I gotta talk to you, outside."

"Why?"

"Old Joe's waiting for us."

"Oh, no," Uriah whispered. "I ain't goin'." Jordan could see that mentioning Old Joe was a mistake.

"Don't you want to hear what happened to me and your mom?"

"You got news about my mama?"

"Yeah. I sure do." This would be the way to get him out. "Meet me by the big tree in front."

"Ain't you goin' with me?"

"In a minute."

"What you gonna do?"

"Never mind right now. Just go!" Jordan waited until he heard Uriah start down the steps, then he slowly opened the door to the master's bedroom. He heard the master's buzzing snore. Holding his breath, his heart racing, Jordan crept in. A tiny shaft of moonlight was coming in through the window and he found the dresser drawer where the master kept the watch. Jordan could barely see anything when he opened it, so he ran his hands around inside. Nothing there but silky cloth, nothing hard or round that felt like a watch. Where was it? He *had* to get that watch! This was his last chance.

He slid his hand over the top of the dresser. It wasn't there either. He crept around the room feeling the tops of the other dressers when his hand brushed against something and knocked it off. He heard the master snort. Jordan's heart did a flip-flop and his legs turned to jelly. He had to get out of here. Now!

"Who's there?" the master mumbled. Jordan bent over and scooted out the open door, hoping that the man had been too sleepy to spot him. But then he heard the bed creak. The master was getting up! Jordan knew that if he tried to make it down the stairs, he'd be chased, so he quickly lay down on Uriah's mat and hoped the master wouldn't light a candle. A moment later he came out the door and stood by Jordan, who put on an act of heavy sleep-breathing.

"Uriah?" he said. "Uriah?" Jordan said nothing, just kept on deep breathing. Then he heard the mistress's voice.

"What's wrong, John?"

"Nothing, Lavinia. Nothing. I thought I heard a noise, but it's nothing."

"Then come back to bed, dear. It was probably just the wind." Jordan pretended to sleep until he heard the master snore. It seemed to take forever. Man, that was close! Uriah was probably going crazy with waiting. In fact Jordan met him on the stairs, coming up as he was going down.

"Why you so slow?" Uriah whispered.

"I'll tell you when we get outside. C'mon!" They sneaked out of the house as quickly as they could and stood in the shadows behind the big tree on the front lawn.

"Where does the master keep his watch?" Jordan asked.

"You talkin' about that watch with the house picture on it?"

"Yeah, that's the one."

"He done give it to somebody for safekeepin' 'cause he thought people been lookin' through his dresser drawers."

Jordan felt dizzy from shock at this news. "Who'd he give it to?"

"A relation of his. I'm not supposed to tell who."

Jordan noticed that Uriah was wearing fancy clothes now. He grabbed Uriah by the neck of his ruffled nightshirt. "Where's that watch?"

"I *ain't* gonna tell."

Time was running out and Old Joe was waiting. If the watch wasn't in the house, Jordan knew he didn't stand a chance of getting it anyway. His throat ached and his eyes blurred with tears. He had lost his mom and his family. The only thing he could do now was to earn those freedom papers. It was all he had left.

"Listen," Jordan said. "Forget the watch. Your family's waiting for you. They need you to come with them to Canada, where you can be free."

"Is my mama there too?"

"No. She isn't."

"What happened to her?"

"She was sold."

"Who bought her?"

"I'm sorry. I don't know."

"Why didn't you ask?" He was crying.

"I just couldn't. I was a slave at that market too, and I would have been whipped if I'd even opened my mouth."

"How come you back here then? You run away?"

Jordan tried to explain to him, as best and as quickly as he could, what had happened to him, being careful not to mention McAllen's name. "Don't you see, Uriah, you could end up in the slave market too. Anytime. But if you went to Canada you'd be free. You could do whatever you want and nobody could ever sell you."

"Nobody ever gonna sell me now."

"How do you know?"

" 'Cause the masta, he be my very own daddy."
When his words sank in, Jordan felt as if somebody'd knocked the wind right out of him.

FOURTEEN

It took Jordan a minute or so to collect his thoughts. After what Uriah had just said, how was he ever going to talk this boy into joining his family? But to get those freedom papers, Jordan had to keep his end of the bargain. The night was hot, and sweat ran down Jordan's neck. A cloud passed over the moon and they stood in the dark. Jordan grabbed Uriah's arm to keep him from taking off.

"Are you sure about what you just said?" Jordan asked.

"The slaves in the quarter, they all knowed it, and tease me. I asked my mama 'bout it a long time ago, and she say it true. And my mama, she don't lie. Then the masta, after he sold my mama, send for me to come and be his servant boy in the big house. He be my daddy, all right. I knows it for sure."

Jordan knew he had to choose his words very carefully to make Uriah understand.

"Look, Uriah," Jordan said, "what about the master's white sons? Are they his servants?"

" 'Course not."

"Why do you suppose that is?" Jordan asked.

" 'Cause they's white. And his wife, she their mama. My mama ain't his wife 'cause that be against the law. My mama used to be housekeeper in the big house, then the mistress had her moved out to the kitchen, then on out to the quarters. The mistress, she the one want my mama sold."

"Okay. I understand," Jordan said. "But the mistress could send you to the trader one day too. You may have the master's blood in your veins, but he's not your real father. No way, man."

"What you mean?"

"Think about this, Uriah," Jordan said. "If he was like a real father, why would he have you sleeping on a mat in the hall instead of giving you a room of your own like his other sons have?"

" 'Cause I'm a nigger."

Jordan grabbed him by the collar. "That's crap! You're a human being, and he ought to treat you like one. If your daddy Seth had a big house do you think you'd be sleeping on a mat in the hall?"

"What you mean 'my daddy Seth'? He not my real daddy. The masta, he be my real daddy."

"Look," Jordan said, "being a real daddy means something different from what you think. It means waiting with the rest of your family, counting the minutes, for you to go with them to freedom. Your real daddy shares whatever he has, like a bed or a whole room if he has it to give. He eats at the same table with you. Tell me something, Uriah, are you eating at the same table with the master?"

" 'Course not," Uriah said. "I stands behind his chair while he eats and shoos away the flies with the long-handle fan. That be one o' my jobs. It be better'n pickin' cotton and livin' at the cabin. I gets to wear good clothes now and eat good food and sleep in a dry, warm place."

Jordan wondered if he'd ever be able to get through to this poor kid. He'd had so little all his life, even the smallest improvement seemed like a gift from heaven. "That's not enough, Uriah, real daddies play with their kids and laugh and joke with them." His throat tightened because he couldn't help thinking about his own dad and how he used to toss a ball to him and smile and tease. "Does the master do those sorts of things with you?"

"The masta, he don't play. Not with me. He just tell me what to do, 'cause he be the masta."

"That's right, he's the master. But he doesn't treat *you* like a son."

Jordan felt as if he were talking to a brick wall, but he kept pushing. "Does the master play with his white kids?"

"He do that all right." Uriah spoke in a quiet voice.

"Do you think he ought to treat his white kids different from you?"

"I never thought about it none." Jordan heard tears in his voice, a good sign.

"Does the master let you call him daddy?"

"I wouldn't dare."

"Does Seth let you call him daddy?"

"Seth, he let me call him daddy same as the others. And, like you say, he do treat me like his own."

"Is the master going to let you go to school same as his white kids?"

"Oh, no. The masta he say it be against the law. I ain't never gonna go to the white folks' tutor." His voice was going soft, and Jordan thought he might be giving in, but he was wrong. "I belongs to Masta Henning," Uriah said, in a trembling half-whisper, "you just leave me be." He wrenched away from Jordan and took off running. Jordan ran after Uriah in the hot stillness, following the sound of his breathing, and when he caught up, he tackled him and held him down on the ground.

"Listen to me, Uriah, and listen hard. Seth wants to take you to a place called Canada where you won't be a slave ever again." Jordan told him all about marching in the chain gang and how Thaddeus had died, and what it was like to stand on the platform in the market. "In Canada," he said, "you can live with your family in your own home and never have to wait on the master or fan the flies off his stupid food ever again. You could even go to school with your brothers and sisters and have your own farm someday." Then Jordan told him about his own mom and Tachelle, and how they were about to move into a fine home in a nice neighborhood. He left out the part about being too scared to go with them—and his decision to join the Cobras.

Uriah stopped struggling and lay still. Jordan could tell that he was trying to make sense of what he'd just told him.

"That sound like a dream too sweet to come true," Uriah said in a soft voice.

"But it's worth a try, isn't it?" Jordan let him sit up. He could tell that Uriah was struggling with himself. To tell the truth, if he were in Uriah's shoes he wasn't sure what he'd do. Here Uriah was, suddenly a lot better off, living close to that soft-spoken white man he looked up to, knowing that he was his flesh and blood. "Uriah," Jordan said, "your own daddy is Seth in every way except his blood. He's the one loving you enough to give you the very best he has. Just come with me. Old Joe is waiting for us. You trust Old Joe, don't you?"

"I reckon I trusts Ol' Joe much as anybody."

"He wants freedom for you too, every bit as much as Seth does," Jordan said. "You believe that, don't you?"

"I believes it, sure enough. But if I goes with you and Ol' Joe, how does I know I gonna get to that Canada place?"

It was a good question. "You'll just have to be

brave and take a chance. My grandpa always told me that nothing good comes without a struggle."

"You say I can go to school like the white folks at Canada?"

"I'm sure of it."

"I'll go then. Jus' first I gotta go back to the big house and do somethin'." But Jordan was afraid that if Uriah ever went back into that house, he'd lose his nerve.

"No, Uriah. If you go back into that house, I'm going to leave, and you'll be a slave the rest of your life. You have to come with me this minute." The cloud floated past the moon and Jordan could see him staring back at Hilltop. A sob caught in Uriah's throat. He got up, grabbed Jordan's hand, and the two of them ran down the lawn to the edge of the woods.

Old Joe was waiting. He hugged them both, then led them through the woods back to the farm. The candle burned in the window. McAllen opened the door and let Uriah and Jordan inside. Old Joe wished them luck, then turned and vanished into the woods.

Mrs. McAllen hugged them, and her husband took an envelope off the kitchen table and handed it to Jordan.

"Your freedom papers," he said. Jordan smiled. He felt as if he'd never worked so hard for anything in his life.

"You can go anywhere or do anything you wish now," said McAllen. "Nobody owns you."

Jordan knew that he was never going to find that watch and that he'd never see his family again. But he did have his freedom papers. He gripped the envelope in both hands. He could leave this house right now a free person. But where would he go? How could he earn enough money to live? And what if he lost his papers or somebody stole them? He could end up in the chain gang again—and not be as lucky next time. The only friends he had in this mixed-up world were Uriah and his family. He made up his mind. If McAllen would let him, he would go to Canada with Uriah.

"I want to go to Canada," Jordan declared.

McAllen nodded. "I don't blame you. I'd do the same if I were you."

After explaining the hardships they'd face on the trip, he agreed to let Jordan go. He told the boys to follow him and to be very quiet. The man stepped outside first, checking to see if the coast was clear, then hurried Uriah and Jordan out the back door and into his barn. To Jordan, the smell of horses and cows was unbelievably strong, and when McAllen closed the door it was so dark that they couldn't see a single thing.

"I can't light the way," McAllen whispered. "Someone might see us and try and break in. Jordan, I'll take your hand and you hang on to Uriah." Jordan stumbled behind McAllen. Uriah clung on to Jordan for dear life. Jordan brushed against something that felt like a horse's tail. Very soon McAllen stopped and Jordan ran a hand along some splintery boards.

"You'll be climbing into this wagon," McAllen whispered. Jordan couldn't see a thing, but he heard breathing. Lots of it. Then the man said, "Uriah, your family is under the hay in the wagon here. You and Jordan will be spending the night in there with them. It'll be hot and uncomfortable and crowded, but you're not to say a word, understand? Not one word. The patrollers have been circling us like crows, watching and listening. You must stay hidden. They wanted to bring their dogs in here to search, but I managed to put them off. The sheriff and his men could come in here with their lanterns and inspect at any time. At sunup I'll be taking you all to a place ten miles from here.

If we make it, the people there will take care of you and send you on your way to the next stop." He paused. "I'll leave you now, but be sure you crawl deep down under the hay so you can't be seen."

Jordan listened as McAllen walked away. Then a man reached out in the dark and put his hand on Jordan's shoulder. He whispered into his ear, "Thank you. God bless you. I'll never forget this." It was Seth.

Seth pulled Uriah and then Jordan into the wagon. Jordan clutched his freedom papers to his chest, being careful, as he slid down, not to poke or step on anyone. It was hot as blazes under that hay-load, and really smelly from all those sweaty bodies. Jordan wasn't exactly looking forward to this trip, but he knew it was the only way out of this hell. If he was going to make it, he'd have to keep his cool.

It wasn't long before silence fell over the wagon. Even Uriah's breathing had that deep, regular sound of sleep. Jordan scrunched up closer to Uriah and tried to settle himself down for a nap. He had just closed his eyes when he suddenly heard ticking near his ear. A watch! It had to be a watch, and its sound came from Uriah. Through Uriah's night-shirt Jordan's fingers closed over a cold round shape that could be only one thing: the master's watch. Its chain seemed to be tied to a cord that hung around Uriah's neck. So the master gave it to a relation for safekeeping! Jordan smiled.

As Jordan gripped the watch through the cloth, the ticking grew louder and louder. The sound filled his ears the way it had when the underpass disappeared and he'd found himself in the swamp woods that first time. The ticking throbbed inside Jordan's head just as it had before, making him dizzy. He felt like he might pass out.

The next thing Jordan knew, he was standing at the corner of Crane and Sutter streets at the top of the underpass. Across the street was Wagner's Pawn Shop and the clock tower. He spun around and saw the street and sidewalk that ran under it. Grandpa's watch was now quietly ticking in the palm of his hand. And he was wearing his regular clothes!

He couldn't believe it. He was back! Back where he belonged! And he had Grandpa's watch! Jordan felt so happy that he whooped and hollered. But he also realized that he'd left Uriah and Seth and Mr.

and Mrs. McAllen, and Old Joe, behind forever, and a terrible sadness overcame him. Those people had been like a family to him. He wished that he could have brought them all along. Tears streamed down his cheeks, knowing the dangers they faced and that there was nothing more he could do to help them.

Wiping away his tears, Jordan stared at the watch's cover. The street lamp lit up the golden Hilltop etching. When he lifted the cover, the watch's hands told the same time as the clock tower across the street: five-thirty, the very time he'd left. How long had he been gone? Hours? Days? Weeks? It had been November 28 when he landed in the woods and met Uriah. He remembered the date because it had been just two days before Mom planned to move to Springdale. And that same evening he'd been on his way to Wagner's Pawn Shop.

Jordan ran around the underpass. No way would he risk going down into it again. He had to return the watch to Grandpa because that's where it belonged. It was his only link to those people he'd grown to love. He speeded up, wondering what in the world he would say to Grandpa.

FIFTEEN

When Jordan finally reached Grandpa's house, he felt a huge relief that he hadn't met up with any of the Cobras or Lobos.

After letting Jordan in, Grandpa sat down in his recliner and picked up the little plastic tray he'd been eating from.

"You're back mighty soon," Grandpa said. "I thought you said you had to be home by six." Jordan couldn't believe his ears. How was it possible that no time at all had gone by? That he was picking up exactly where he'd left off?

"Want to join me for some supper? Or are you still having pizza with your mother?" Grandpa asked. If he'd been missing for several days, Grandpa would have mentioned it. Instead he was acting as if nothing at all had happened.

"Got one just like this in the freezer," Grandpa told him. "I could put it in the microwave and heat it up in three minutes."

Jordan decided not to let on. "No thanks, I don't have time. By the way, Grandpa, what's today's date, anyway?"

"November twenty-eighth. Why?"

"Just wondered," Jordan replied. He'd guessed right. No time had passed. But he couldn't begin to tell Grandpa what had happened to him. In the first place he probably wouldn't believe him, and in the second place he didn't want Grandpa to know that he'd taken his watch. Jordan wanted to put it back before he noticed it was gone. "I came to borrow one of those *National Geographics* on your dresser, Grandpa. We're supposed to write a paper on some foreign country for social studies." This part was true. Luckily he had remembered the assignment. It gave him just the excuse he needed. But he hated having to be so sneaky. He had thought everything would be great once he got back to his own time, but he still felt uneasy. Still scared every minute he'd be found out, and afraid of getting trapped by the Cobras or the Lobos.

"Sure, help yourself, but let me see which one you take, because I'll want it back when you're through." Grandpa put his tray down on a pile of newspapers and slowly got up. Oh, no! He was going to follow him into the bedroom! In a panic Jordan hurried to Grandpa's dresser just ahead of him and quickly slipped the watch back into its box. He was closing the lid when Grandpa walked over to him.

"Glad you're showing an interest in that watch," Grandpa said. He must have seen him put the lid back on. Stay cool, Jordan told himself.

"It belonged to your namesake, you know," said Grandpa.

"My namesake?" Jordan said. "I thought this watch came down to you from Uriah Henning. My name's not Uriah."

"No, but Uriah changed his name to Jordan when he found a set of freedom papers made out to Jordan Henning. The odd thing was, he found them in a hay wagon just before he left for Canada on the underground railroad." Jordan felt the blood rush up to his head, then back down to his feet.

He took a deep breath to keep from passing out. *His* freedom papers! The ones he'd left in the wagon!

Jordan tried to act casual. "How did Uriah get the watch?"

"The story is that Uriah had the watch on him because the master gave it to him for safekeeping. He was afraid somebody was trying to steal it from him. The person who talked Uriah into leaving wouldn't let him take that watch back to the big house. Told him he had to leave that very minute or not at all. So the watch stayed with Uriah for the rest of his life. And it came down to me through four generations."

Jordan's knees felt weak, as if they could buckle under him any minute, and his voice shook. "Who was that person who talked Uriah into going to Canada?"

"We don't know. That part of the story has been lost over the years."

Fighting dizziness, Jordan asked another question. "What happened to Uriah after he found the papers?" Grandpa didn't seem to notice how strange Jordan's voice sounded.

"Well, he and his family made the trip all the way

from the deep South to Canada on the Underground Railroad. Had a number of very close calls. But they all made it except for Uriah's little sister, who died from a snakebite, and a brother who caught the fever and had to be left behind. None of the family ever saw that brother again or heard what happened to him. Uriah hung on to those freedom papers even after he got to Canada. He was afraid he might need them someday if Canada ever changed its laws. He never did of course, but he went by the name of Jordan from then on." Grandpa smiled and patted his grandson's shoulder. "You come from a long line of brave people, Jordan."

"You're right," Jordan said quietly. Grandpa had no way of knowing how well he knew this. There was a lump the size of a baseball in his throat and he ached to tell Grandpa what had happened, but he couldn't. Not yet. Maybe someday.

Grandpa helped Jordan pick out a *National Geographic*, one about Africa. He reminded Jordan of Seth. Both were sweet-natured and would give you anything they had. Right then he made up his mind that he'd never lie to Grandpa or steal from him ever again.

"You be careful now," Grandpa told Jordan

when he walked out the door. "Those streets can be mean after dark. I'm going to phone your mama and tell her you're on your way and to watch out for you."

"Thanks." Jordan took off running. He couldn't wait to see Mom and Tachelle. He hoped they'd saved him some pizza! Nothing could stop him now! In just a few minutes he'd be home!

Suddenly somebody popped out of the shadows and planted himself in front of Jordan. It was King. And right behind him stood his right-hand man, a Cobra called Hood. Jordan felt as if fear was paralyzing him. At that moment his thoughts were so confused that anything he said might come out wrong. And these were the last people in the world he wanted to see right now.

"You runnin' the wrong way, bro," said King. Hood grabbed one of Jordan's arms and King held the other. "You got a short memory, homeboy. Seems like less'n hour ago we was talkin' Baker's parking lot at six."

"And accordin' to King here, you was gonna bring money," said Hood. "So what's the story? You got the cash?"

"My plan didn't work out," Jordan said. He was

plotting his escape, just as he had done in that not-so-long-ago world. When he looked at these two guys now, he saw Travis and Master Henning and the paddyrollers. King and Hood sent guys like him out to do their dirty work. Jordan knew what he had to say to them, and what would happen when he said it.

Jordan took a deep breath. "I want out," he said. His voice was loud and clear; the awestruck quiver in it was gone. Nobody was going to make a slave out of him. Never. Not after what he'd been through.

King and Hood said nothing for a few seconds, then they both tightened their grip on him and twisted his arms. They said, "You what?"

"Like I said, I'm out. Free."

"I told you this nigger's a softheaded punk," Hood said to King, "but you wouldn't listen. If we don't take care o' him quick, man, he gonna squeal." They twisted his arms even tighter.

"Since you ain't our homie no more," said King, "you is a fair game nigger. You comin' with us, boy." The two of them dragged Jordan the three blocks to Baker's parking lot. His arms were killing him. Jordan wasn't sure he would live through what they would do to him. Once more he wondered if he'd ever see his family again. Jordan prayed too. He couldn't help thinking that maybe it would have been better if he'd stayed with Uriah and his family, but that choice was lost in time.

All the Cobras were there, bunched around a pickup truck. A van drove up and parked next to it. Jordan guessed that it belonged to the gun dealer. There was no escape. King told the others Jordan wanted out. Then he told everybody that they were going to teach him what they did to those who showed such "disrespect." By this time Jordan was close to passing out. He was so scared that he even considered changing his mind. But then thoughts of Seth and Old Joe and Mr. McAllen and Uriah flashed through his mind. They'd risked their lives for freedom and wouldn't have changed their minds. Whatever happened, he wouldn't either.

The Cobras took metal pipes out of the pickup and several of them slipped on brass knuckles. All of a sudden King gave Jordan a shove that sent him reeling between two lines of Cobras. Something bashed into his face and whacked his shoulders. The pain was terrible. His back and legs felt broken, and blood filled his mouth. He told himself to stay on his feet and look for a chance to run.

A savage kick in the stomach stopped him cold. The pain was so intense that he couldn't move. Then Jordan heard a gun go off, so close that it was deafening. Something like an electric shock tore down his arm and across his back. Before he blacked out, he realized that he'd been shot.

SIXTEEN

Jordan woke up in a white bed with a blue curtain all around it. He must have said something because a woman in a nurse's uniform popped through the curtain and stood by him. She felt his wrist and looked at her watch. Pain rose up in waves all through Jordan's body. Then he noticed the tubes taped to his arm.

"Where am I?" he whispered.

"In the recovery room at St. Mary's Hospital," the nurse said. "You got out of surgery about an hour ago."

"My mom. Where's my mom?"

"She's waiting in your room. You'll see her in a few minutes."

"Where's Tachelle?"

"Who?"

"Tachelle. My little sister." He fell asleep before he heard the nurse's reply.

The next time Jordan woke up he was in a room with pale green walls and a venetian blind at the window. Standing by his bed was Mom, looking down at him with her uptilted eyes. For a moment he thought it was Clara. How alike they were! She squeezed his hand. It was like a dream come true. The pain was bad and his eyes went blurry with tears as he squeezed her hand back. Grandpa stood by her and smiled at him.

"Where's Tachelle?" Jordan whispered.

Tears were streaming down Mom's face. "She's in school. She'll come and see you tonight. Thank God you're alive!" In the bed next to Jordan, a boy about his age was watching a television set that hung from the ceiling.

"The doctors tell us you're going to be all right," said Grandpa. "Bullet just missed your heart."

"If Grandpa hadn't called me to watch for you after you left his place," Mom said, "I wouldn't have known anything was wrong. When you didn't show up, I went out and looked for you. It didn't take long." Mom stopped and wiped her eyes with a tissue and sobbed, then continued in a shaky voice. "I was driving along watching for you when I saw a police car parked ahead of me with its lights flashing and a group of people staring at something on the ground. I stopped the car and got out. Two bodies were stretched out on the sidewalk and a policeman was radioing for an ambulance. When I saw that one of those bodies was you, I—"

"Two?" Jordan whispered. He couldn't believe what he'd heard. "Two? Who besides me?"

"Somebody by the name of Phil Bromley. He was killed."

Phil Bromley was Hood. "What happened?" he whispered.

But Mom was crying so hard that she couldn't go on talking.

Grandpa put his arm around her and told him the rest. "According to the police, somebody fired two shots, probably aimed at you, but whoever did the shooting missed on the second one and got Bromley instead. They've arrested somebody named Daniel Holden and charged him with second-degree murder."

Daniel Holden! King!

"Did you know those people?" Mom asked.

"Yes," Jordan whispered.

"Oh, Jordan!" she cried, "how could you get mixed up with something like that?"

"At first they were kinda nice to me. And I needed money."

"What for? I'm able to buy you everything you need."

"Except airfare to go see Daddy. Why won't you let me go see him?"

Mom patted his arm. "We'll talk about that later, I promise. Get some sleep now."

"You're a mighty lucky fella, I'd say," said Grandpa. Lucky? Well, maybe. But every part of Jordan's body hurt so bad that it felt like he was on fire. Then a nurse came in and gave him a shot. In no time at all he was asleep.

After Jordan got out of the hospital, he moved into the new Springdale house with Mom and Tachelle.

Soon after, Jordan and Grandpa sat at a desk in the living room of their new home. Since he couldn't visit his dad now or talk to him on the phone, Jordan decided to write him a letter. But the words just wouldn't come and he needed Grandpa's help. Jordan's left arm was still in a sling and there was a brace on his neck so that he couldn't turn his head. When those things came off next week he'd feel human again. He stared at the two words on the sheet of paper.

Dear Dad.

After chewing on his pencil, he finally wrote, *Mom told me where you are.*

"Grandpa," he said, "how do you spell prison?" Since Mom had to work, Grandpa was staying with Jordan till he got well enough to go back to school. He was helping him keep up with his classes at Springdale Middle School.

"P-r-i-s-o-n."

"No *z*?"

"No *z*."

"Why not? It sounds like it should have a *z*."

"A lot of words aren't spelled the way they sound."

Jordan looked up at Grandpa and smiled. Man! Talk about smart. Grandpa knew all sorts of things. "I want to tell him why I can't visit him now like I'd planned. What else should I say?"

Grandpa said, "You might want to tell him that

you miss him and think about him and hope to see him someday."

"Okay. I'll tell him that. Do you think he's lonely and misses me?" asked Jordan.

"Of course he misses you. He loves you. That won't ever change."

Jordan gripped his pencil and wrote, *I hope you aren't too lonely and that you'll write and let me know how you're doing.* When Mom finally told him where Daddy was, Jordan couldn't believe it.

"Grandpa, why did Daddy do that fraud thing? You know, cheating people? He was always so nice."

"Well, Jordan, he just let himself get caught up in a sort of trap. Kind of like what you just went through." Did Grandpa know about traveling back in time with the watch? Had it ever happened to him? Jordan held his breath.

"Some people set a trap for folks like us when they keep us from doing our very best. They think we have no right to set our sights high. They put us down because of our slave history and our race, and pretty soon some of us believe them. That's the trap." Jordan understood what Grandpa was saying, but couldn't help feeling a little disappointed. No time travel.

"But how did that happen to Daddy?"

Grandpa sighed. "Well, I think it went something like this. He couldn't find whatever it was he was looking for in life, so he just gave up on himself. He didn't want to go to school at night like your mama did or maybe try and learn new skills. He was probably pretty desperate when this bunch of con men took him in and offered him a deal that sounded too good to be true. He fell for it. You know the end of the story."

"Yeah, I guess I can understand that." King had sweet-talked him into joining the Cobras, then almost killed him. "I wonder why King did what he did."

"Probably lots of reasons, none of them good. Grew up poor, quit school, then couldn't find work. He wanted to be a big, important guy. Running a gang gave him a position in life."

"So he fell into his own trap."

"Exactly. And dragged others down with him."

Jordan had never thought about King in that way before. He'd admired him, even hoped to be a little bit like him. There was something about all of this that reminded him of how Uriah had looked up to the master. Jordan knew this was something he'd be thinking about for a long time.

"See if you can wrap up that letter so we can get it into today's mail," said Grandpa. "In the meantime I'll go into the kitchen and make some popcorn."

"Sure, Grandpa." Jordan stared at what he had written and added two more sentences: *I almost got killed because I joined a gang. I think harder now about the choices I make.*

Jordan got up from the desk and joined Grandpa in the kitchen. When the popcorn was done, Grandpa set the bowl down on the kitchen table, then brought the checkers game in from the living room.

"Thought it was time we had a little fun."

"Good idea, Grandpa." Jordan jumped up and ran to the desk. "I'll be right back." He added one more sentence to his letter: *I love you, Dad.*

Back at the kitchen table, Grandpa and Jordan lined up their checkers.

"Every place you go," said Grandpa, "people will try to put you down and hold you back. Just be on your guard and fight for your rights." He looked down at the checkerboard. "Your move," he said.

Jordan grinned. It sure was.

For many Christmases and Thanksgivings afterward Grandpa showed off the Hilltop watch. Jordan never told him about having taken it that night or what had happened to him at that street underpass. Maybe he never would. After all, who'd believe him?

Author's Note

While doing research for *Trapped Between the Lash and the Gun,* I found the first-hand accounts of slaves to be the most heartrending material I had ever read. I came away not only admiring the people's strength to survive, but also their ability to go on and somehow build lives for themselves and their families. But something else haunted me. It was what *wasn't* said—the crime of slavery left a legacy that few talked about. Even after freedom was won, slavery continued to rob most black people of the self-esteem and hope that white Americans took for granted. Doors were routinely closed in black faces. Even today, those doors of opportunity are only partially open. Somehow I knew that I had to write a story that brought the world of slavery and the present-day black experience together.

One might think this a strange subject for a white woman to write about. Especially someone who grew up the privileged daughter of a successful small-town doctor. As a child and teenager in the 1930's, I attended a nearly all-white school. I was acquainted with the few black children in my class, but real friendship between us never developed. At that time it hadn't occurred to me to question why black folks lived in their own neighborhood, or why socializing between the races in our town was unheard of. It was not until the civil rights movement in the 1960's that I began to realize, and to truly feel, the terrible injustices suffered by African-Americans in our country. As a storyteller, I am always searching for meaningful themes. The history of black people in this country gave me what I was looking for, and lit the spark for Jordan Scott's fictional journey.

Sometime after Dial Books agreed to publish my manuscript, I received a phone call from a distant cousin in California whom I had never met. Nor indeed had I ever heard of him. He had done extensive geneology research on my father's side of the family, and sent me documents proving that my great-grandmother, whom I had never been able to locate, had been an ex-slave named Jane. She had been given her Kentucky plantation master's surname, Embry. Jane Embry had six children, all boys, one of whom was my grandfather, my own father's father. From what my cousin was able to piece together, Jane's first son was born into slavery around 1835 and was granted his freedom by Jane's owner in 1842 for a fee of three hundred dollars. Later Jane was freed and, the 1860 Kentucky census tells us, headed a household that included my grandfather and four of his brothers. By that time the second-oldest son had moved to Ohio. A recently discovered letter names Joel Walker as the father of Jane's children. He and Jane were never married. In the 1860 Kentucky census (see page 185), Jane and her sons' race was listed as "mulatto," meaning a mix of black and white. During the early part of the Civil War, Jane and her five sons migrated to Kansas. Since they were sufficiently light-skinned to "pass," the sons were listed as white in later Kansas censuses.

I was astounded, to say the least. And fascinated. Questions dogged me. Did my father know? If he did, why did he conceal this amazing history from his immediate family? On my grandfather's death certificate, false names were given for his parents. Since my father filled out that death certificate, I wonder if he deliberately lied or if he believed these names to be the real ones. Since he is dead, I will probably never know.

The fact that my family history was so carefully hidden is a sad commentary on the attitude toward black people after the Civil War and well into the twentieth century. Those years were filled with Ku Klux Klan activities and lynchings, to say nothing of barriers to careers and ordinary services. A black person during that time could not rent a motel room, eat in a restaurant, or try on clothes in stores run by white people. Public schools in the South were racially separate, and certainly inferior for black children. Today, though public schools admit all children, some have become nearly all black or all white because of their locations. Too often, neighborhoods are still segregated. Before the 1960's, black students were denied entrance into many universities and colleges. If his "Negro blood" had been known back in 1907, I doubt that my father would have been accepted into medical school.

I realize that if it had not been concealed, this ancestral history would have meant fewer rights for me and my family. My people likely did what they felt they had to do during troubled times. Still, it saddens and angers me that my African-American heritage could close doors to opportunity and basic rights. And still can.

I am proud to be the great-granddaughter of that brave woman Jane Embry. In her fifties, with her five sons and a granddaughter, she migrated to a wild and dangerous part of the country to start a new life. It makes me happy to know that during her lifetime the Kansas territory was voted into the Union as a "free state," a place where none of its citizens would ever be enslaved.

Transcript of Emancipation Deed for Wade Embry (author's great-uncle):

MADISON COUNTY DEED BOOK Z, Page 338

April 1842

Know all men by these presents, that I Talton Embry of the County of Madison and State of Kentucky, for and in consideration of the sum of three hundred dollars, to me in hand paid, the receipt whereof is hereby acknowledged, I do by these presents emancipate & set free, my negro boy slave named Wade, son of my negro woman named Jane. Said boy Wade is about nine years old next October, of a yellow complexion. For the consideration aforesaid I do hereby emancipate him, and transfer to him all the rights and privileges as same as if he had been born free.

Given under my hand & seal this 22nd day of April, in the year, 1842.

Talton Embry

The above is a portion of the actual document.

On the facing page is a photo of a page from the 1860 federal census for Kentucky. The Civil War had not yet begun and Kentucky still had persons who were legally enslaved. The following year, despite a continuing strong pro-slavery element, most Kentuckians would fight on the side of the Northern forces.

Wade Embry and his mother, Jane, had both been freed earlier by the purchase of Emancipation Deeds. From this census document we know that at this time Jane worked as a washerwoman and headed a household of five males and one female. None of the family is listed as being married or having attended school. Their real estate holding received a value of $400, and they had a personal estate worth $50.

Both Jane, at age 49, and Wade, at age 23, are listed as being unable to read and write. The family's "color," meaning race, is given as "mulatto," a term which refers to a person of mixed black and white parentage. In *Trapped Between the Lash and the Gun,* the character known as Uriah would most likely have been classified under this term. For unknown reasons, the census specifically notes only the race of those few free mulattos. Later censuses (those recorded after the family moved to Kansas) list most of these same family members as white.

Toliver Embry, then 17 years of age, is the author's grandfather. *Within a single generation* Toliver's son would become a respected small-town doctor and the father of two children. His daughter was named Arvella. She grew up believing her family's racial heritage to be exclusively white, not knowing about her connection to Jane, Wade, or any of the members of her family listed on this page. In later years, Arvella became a wife, mother, writer, teacher, and the author of *Trapped Between the Lash and the Gun.*

SCHEDULE 1.—Free Inhabitants in _the Town of Richmond_ in the County of _Madison_ State of _Kentucky_ enumerated by me, on the _4th_ day of _June_ 1860. _Wm Biggerstaff_ Ass't Marshal.

Post Office _Richmond Ky_

		The name of every person whose usual place of abode on the first day of June, 1860, was in this family.	Age	Sex	Color	Profession, Occupation, or Trade of each person, male and female, over 15 years of age.	Value of Real Estate.	Value of Personal Estate.	Place of Birth, Naming the State, Territory, or County.	Married within the year.	Attended School within the year.	Persons over 20 y'rs of age who cannot read & write.	Whether deaf and dumb, blind, insane, idiotic, pauper, or convict.	
1	2	3	4	5	6	7	8	9	10	11	12	13	14	
49	49	Samuel Strasher	45	M		Hatter	700	100	Virginia					1
		Ann " "	39	F					Madison City					2
		E Jane " "	23	F		Common School teacher		300	" "					3
		John R " "	20	M		Asst Seller Business			" "					4
		William E " "	19	M		Clerk in Grocery			" "					5
		Mary E " "	13	F					" "					6
		James H " "	12	M					" "		1			7
		Hiram L " "	10	M					" "		1			8
		Eliza " "	8	F					" "		1			9
		Horace L " "	4	M					" "					10
50	50	E R McCreary	56	M		Farmer	3800	8000	Clerk City					11
		Sabrina " "	50	F					Madison City					12
		James B " "	21	M		Farmer	4000	1000	" "					13
51	51	Emily Grant	30	F			5000	2500	" "					14
		Emily " "	9	F					" "		1			15
		Margaret " "	7	F					" "					16
		John " "	4	M					" "					17
		Mary Brown	32	F					" "					18
		R Maxwell	32	M		Harness Maker			New York					19
		Martha " "	25	F					Madison City					20
		Ann E " "	3	F					" "					21
		Mildred E " "	1	F					" "					22
52	52	C H Donaldson	48	M		Hatter		1500	Maryland					23
		John A McCauley	24	M		Silver Smith		3500	Fayette City					24
53	53	Elizabeth Poles	58	F			600	200	Connecticut					25
		Caroline " "	35	F					Fayette City					26
		Sarah " "	32	F					Indiana					27
54	54	Silas J Green	45	M		Clerk in the Bank	5000	2000	Madison City					28
55	55	Albert Mackey	45	M	M	Barber	3000	3000	Lincoln City			M		29
		Joseph Divison	85	M	M	Farm Laborer			Virginia			M		30
56	56	Jane Embry	49	F	M	Washerwoman	400	50	Madison City			M		31
		Mide " "	25	M	M	Say Laborer			" "			M		32
		Oliver " "	17	M	M	" "			" "					33
		William " "	12	M	M				" "					34
		Charles " "	9	M	M				" "					35
		John " "	6	M	M				" "					36
		Drucilla " "	2	F	M				" "					37
57	57	P P Ballard	48	M		Hotel Keeper	100	4000	" "					38
		Mary A " "	41	F					" "					39
														40

No. white males, _14_   No. colored males, _7_   No. foreign born, ___   No. blind, ___   _6800 57500_   No. idiotic, ___

No. white females, _14_   No. colored females, _2_   No. deaf and dumb, ___   No. insane, ___   No. paupers, ___   No. convicts, ___